COCKROACH COOTIES

MVFOL

by LAURENCE YEP

D1017986

Hyperion Paperbacks for Children New York

Copyright © 2000 by Laurence Yep

All rights reserved.

No part of this book may be reproduced or transmitted in any form or by any means, electronic or mechanical, including photocopying, recording, or by any information storage and retrieval system, without written permission from the publisher. For information address Hyperion Books for Children, 114 Fifth Avenue, New York, New York 10011-5690.

Printed in the United States of America

First paperback edition, 2001

3 5 7 9 10 8 6 4

This book is set in 12.5-point Galliard.

Library of Congress Cataloging-in-Publication Data

Yep, Laurence.

Cockroach cooties / Laurence Yep.—1st ed.

p. cm.

Summary: Teddy and his little brother, Bobby, devise strategies using bugs to defeat the school bully.

ISBN 0-7868-0487-4 (hc.).—ISBN 0-7868-2565-0 (lib.).— ISBN 0-7868-1338-5 (pbk.).

[1. Brothers—Fiction. 2. Bullies—Fiction. 3. Insects—Fiction. 4. Chinese Americans—Fiction.]

I. Title.

PZ7 . Y44Ck   2000

[Fic]—dc21   99-36771

Visit www.hyperionchildrensbooks.com

To my father-in-law, "Bugs" Ryder,
or Raymond Ryder, as he is known
to his unsuspecting neighbors

Author's Note

One of the hazards of marrying a nature poet like Joanne Ryder is that I never know what I'll find when I come home from a trip. I once returned to find our refrigerator filled with mealworms and our home with crickets and snails. (At least the last-named were quiet and easy to catch if they escaped.)

I never thought I'd be living with a real-life Bobby. Joanne only confessed to me when it was already too late that her nickname was "Spider" Ryder.

One

My day was turning out perfect. That morning Sister Marie canceled the spelling test. At recess I'd just made a great trade in baseball cards. For lunch, the cafeteria made hot dogs and spaghetti, my favorite.

And when I went out into the school yard for noon recess, the sun was shining. It hardly ever made it past all the buildings in Chinatown. So I just stood there and soaked up the warmth.

Then Bobby and his friends moved past. If anyone knew how to destroy a perfect day, it was my little brother. I started to frown, but he was too busy bragging.

"And I help the Bug Lady with the frass," he said as he passed me.

I rolled my eyes. Not that again.

"What's that?" his friend asked.

I could see Bobby lean forward and whisper in his ear.

The friend giggled. "You know so many words for that stuff."

I sighed. My little brother certainly did. Father called those five-dollar words. That's how much Mother fined Father when he used synonyms for *frass*. Lucky for Bobby that neither of our parents knew what *frass* or his other five-dollar words really meant.

Suddenly I heard Arnie's roar. Arnie had a big voice—as in monster big. Not just Frankenstein big. *Godzilla* big. You could hear his voice across the school yard.

"You're weird, Bobby," Arnie said.

"It takes one to know one," Bobby said.

Everyone thinks Bobby is the sweet one of us. That's why everyone likes him. When my grandmother talks about him, she always beams.

Me, I'm the normal one. I talk back and get into

fights. When my grandmother mentions me, she just shakes her head and sighs.

However, right now Bobby was sounding like . . . well, me.

"Who you calling weird, Bug Boy?" Arnie demanded.

I was sorry to lose the sun on my face, but I turned away from it and from my brother. I started to walk away.

Big brothers owed it to little brothers to prepare them for real life. Bobby had to learn how to deal with problems on his own. Especially when problems were as big as Arnie.

At nine, Arnie was the same age as me, but he'd been held back a year. He could barely read and write his name in English. It wasn't because he was stupid, though. In Chinese school, he was one of the stars. He'd just cut classes too much.

This would be his second year in the second grade. Bobby wasn't very big for eight. Arnie could have made three of him.

"You . . . you frass head," Bobby answered.

His friends giggled.

"What's that mean?" Arnie demanded. His voice got real angry.

"Go look it up, Fewmets Breath," Bobby snapped.

That was a new one on me. Even *I* hadn't been called that. Where did Bobby pick up this stuff? I made a note to look it up if I could ever figure out how to spell it.

However, Bobby must have explained that one to his friends, too. They burst out laughing.

"I don't know what it means, but it doesn't sound so good," Arnie snarled.

"Hey, let me go!" Bobby protested.

I shut my eyes and tried to shut my ears. Bobby didn't have the talent to be nasty. Anyone can mouth off. The trick is to get away with it.

"I'm going to teach you a lesson, Bug Boy," Arnie growled.

"Ow, that hurts," Bobby said.

I looked around. The nun in charge was Sister Philomena. She was nice, but she was a little hard of hearing. Right now she was busy helping some first graders jump rope. She wouldn't have heard World War Two if it happened in the school yard.

I suppose I could have gotten her, but then I would be tattling. And I was no tattler.

"Teddy, help!" Bobby called in a strangled voice.

Normally I didn't take orders from Bobby. I didn't believe in that brotherly love stuff, either. Frankly, I think it's overrated.

However, there was one part of brotherhood I took seriously. In fact, it was the privilege of all big brothers. Nobody could do serious damage to my little brother except me.

I muttered a good-bye to my perfect day as I spun around. Arnie was even bigger than I remembered. At the moment he was busy trying to press Bobby flat as a sheet against a brick wall.

Somehow I managed to get my jelly legs moving in that direction. With each step, though, Arnie got bigger. And his hair was gelled so it swept up like a wave on top of his head. That made him seem even taller.

"Let him go, Arnie," I said, tapping him on the shoulder.

Arnie twisted his ugly face around. "Stay out of this, Teddy. It's none of your business."

"If you pick on my little brother, you make it my

business," I said. I kicked him right behind his knee. He looked surprised when his leg gave out. He toppled over just like a tree.

"You're going to die, Teddy," Arnie roared. I jumped on his back and tried to put a wrestling hold on him like I'd seen on television. Arnie, though, was a lot stronger than me. It was like sitting on Godzilla after he'd just sat on an anthill.

I bucked up and down for a moment. The next moment I was flying onto the asphalt.

"Fight, fight!" the kids chanted excitedly.

Arnie was so mad that he couldn't talk. He just made little strangling noises as he pounded his fists together. He looked ready to break every bone in my body.

"Get Sister," Bobby told one of his friends.

However, Sister Philomena would come too late. I'd seen Arnie get this upset once. It had taken two nuns to pull him away. By then the other kid had a broken rib. Dear, sweet Sister Philomena couldn't have handled Arnie on her own.

There was only one thing to do. I rolled over on my stomach and hit my own face against the ground. Then I sat up.

As I'd hoped, Arnie was so startled that he stopped. The next moment I could taste something salty. It was my blood.

I figured it was a good trade-off: a bloody nose was better than a broken rib.

"You're even weirder than your brother," Arnie said, scratching his head.

"What's going on?" Sister Philomena demanded, shoving her way through the ring of children.

"Arnie was picking on me, and Teddy came to the rescue," Bobby said. He sounded a little surprised himself.

"He kicked me," Arnie said, pointing at me. "I never touched him."

Sister Philomena drew her eyebrows together. "Then why does he have the bloody nose?"

As Sister Philomena grabbed Arnie's collar, he protested, "But I didn't do anything."

"Tell that to Sister Principal," she said as she dragged him off.

"You're a dead man, Teddy," Arnie yelled.

I didn't doubt that for one moment.

Bobby was the first one to get to me. "Thank you, Teddy." He handed me a tissue.

I tore off a strip and rolled it up. Then I plugged it into my nose. "I've been saving that trick," I said. My voice sounded a little funny with a nose plug. "The trouble is, you only get away with that once." And now Arnie-zilla would be after me.

Two

For once, I hated it when I heard the school bell ring at three-thirty. I knew what was coming. I figured there was safety in numbers. "Want to shoot some baskets?" I asked Ollie.

"Uh . . . no. I got to do homework," Ollie said.

I turned to Cousin Roderick. "What about it, cuz?"

"I got homework, too," he said.

I'd never known either of them to crack a book. "Good idea. I'll do my homework with you."

Ollie held up his hands. "No, I got to go to the

9

Laundromat first. My mom wants me to do the dirty clothes."

Cousin Roderick shook his head. "Yeah, sorry. I got chores, too."

I was getting desperate. "Well, we could walk home together. You know—safety in numbers."

Ollie and Cousin Roderick backed away like I had the plague. "You picked the fight, not us," Ollie said. "That was like kicking King Kong in the shin."

"He was picking on Bobby," I said.

"Well, Bobby's not our brother," Cousin Roderick said.

"Well, he's your cousin," I said, but the pair of cowards had already broken into a run.

They were heading for the side door to the school. I thought of galloping after them. With a little luck, we'd be a real blur. Arnie might even hit one of them by mistake.

After all, that's what Ollie and Cousin Roderick would have done if they were in my situation. But I wasn't either of them.

I made a note to myself to get a better class of friends.

Picking up my book bag, I headed for the front

door. At least I'd be in hollering distance of Sister Principal.

I paused at the big plate-glass doors. I could see a bus. There wasn't any sign of Arnie, though.

Suddenly my legs got wobbly. I felt just like a prisoner going to the electric chair. Would one broken rib be enough for Arnie?

Taking a breath, I opened the door and stepped outside.

"He's not here," Bobby said.

I nearly jumped out of my skin. Turning, I saw him leaning against the side of the building.

"What are you doing here?" I asked.

He straightened up. "I thought I'd wait for you."

I shook my head at his stupidity. "You could have gotten beaten up."

He shrugged. "After what you did, it's the least I could do."

Sometimes I didn't know whether to hug him or slug him. "Don't be dumb. How could you stop Arnie?" I asked. "You'd be some bodyguard."

"I know I'm not a fighter," he admitted. "But I thought I could take a few punches for you."

I sighed. He might not be the best little brother

11

in the world, but he was all I had. "Yeah, maybe he would have worn himself out hitting you."

He grinned. "We have to get Mom's birthday present anyway. Her banquet is tomorrow."

"But we'd better watch out for Arnie," I said, glancing around.

We turned from Stockton down the steep hill. There were some tourists with cameras, sunglasses, and hats. They were puffing as they climbed the steep slope.

One of them paused and wiped the sweat from his forehead. "Doesn't this hill ever stop?" he asked.

A woman read from a tourist brochure. "That's why they put cable cars going up them."

We left them struggling up the sidewalk. The street stalls were near Grant Avenue. They were really only big, wide, shallow cabinets on the side of the buildings. At night, the owners just closed the doors and locked them.

Though the stalls were smaller than a regular store, they were still very useful. They sold most everything anyone could want. There were post-cards for the tourists, but there was also candy in rows of glass jars. The thin bright-red strips of candied ginger were piled in one. In another was a mound of sweet preserved plums.

The owner of that particular stall lowered his racing form. "Ver-ree tas-tee," he assured us.

My mouth started to water just looking at all the different treats. "Mother likes sweets. Let's get her some of these."

Bobby had my number, though. "How much would Mom really get and how much would you?"

"Well, you got to sample them," I said defensively.

"Yeah, right," Bobby said. He walked slowly along the stall, examining every item.

On the lower shelves were the toys. Papier-mâché snakes slithered across the board. I picked up one. The snake was jointed so it seemed to wriggle in my hand. "Let's get one of these," I said.

"Ver-ree edu-ca-shun-al," the stall owner promised.

Bobby shook his head. "I think Mom's had her fill of reptiles."

For his last birthday, I had bought Bobby a pet alligator, Oscar. I'd meant it as a prank. Only it had backfired. Bobby had liked it, but it had made all sorts of trouble when it got loose.

"Mom just said I couldn't buy anything that could bite back," I said. "This is safe."

Bobby, though, continued to inspect the stall. "I'm not chipping in for a fake snake."

I flipped the snake over and looked at the price tag. Since I had only a dime in my pocket, I needed his money. Bobby was not only the sweet one. He was also the cheap one. He still had almost every penny he'd ever gotten.

There were wooden popguns shaped like short canes. I grabbed one off the shelf and pushed the cork into the muzzle.

The gun came in two pieces. I held the barrel with one hand and pulled back the handle with the other. When I shoved the pieces together, the cork shot out with a loud pop and then dangled by its string.

"Ver-ree han-dee," the stall owner said.

Proudly I showed it to Bobby. "Mother would really like this. She can get those hard-to-reach cockroaches."

Bobby turned back to the shelves. "You'd wear it out before her birthday."

He was probably right, but he was still the most

14

annoying little brother. "Well, what do you think she'd like?" I asked in frustration.

Bobby paused and selected a scarf. "Maybe this." It feels real soft. When he spread it open, we could see the Golden Gate Bridge.

"Great," I said.

"Ver-ree love-lee," the owner agreed. He seemed to have a phrase for each item.

Bobby crouched so he could see the price tag and frowned. "It's also too expensive." Folding it up carefully, he put it back.

Finally the owner decided to get more involved. "Who this for?" he asked, getting up from his stool.

"Our mother," I said.

He pursed his lips as he nodded his head. Slowly he shuffled along his stall and then solemnly selected an ashtray. Inside was a painting of a cable car. "Ver-ree use-ful."

If I had my own money, I could have done all my Christmas shopping in this amount of time. "What about this?" I asked Bobby.

The owner helpfully held it so Bobby could see the cable car.

"Mom doesn't smoke," he reminded me.

15

The owner put back the ashtray and folded his arms as he pondered the problem.

Suddenly Bobby stooped. From a large can on the sidewalk, neon pink, yellow, and green hands waved at us. "She'd like this." He examined the hands and then pulled out a pink one. One side of the stem said: OFFICIAL SOUVENIR OF CHINA-TOWN, U.S.A. The back said: MADE IN HOBOKEN, NEW JERSEY. So much for authentic Chinatown souvenirs.

I scratched my head. "A plastic back scratcher? I think the popgun is a better idea."

"Last night I heard her ask Dad to scratch her back," Bobby said. "She got a rash from something Aunt Ethel cooked."

Aunt Ethel was always experimenting with new recipes. I'd learned to eat something before any of her meals.

"Are you sure?" I asked.

"Positive," Bobby said.

Bobby was the thoughtful one. Mom always liked his presents. Some of mine made her frown.

"Okay," I said, and dug my dime out of my pocket.

"I thought we were going to go halves?" Bobby said.

"This is all I got," I said.

"No wonder you wanted to share the present this year." Bobby sighed. He almost always forgave me.

As he paid the owner, I asked, "Can you wrap it?"

The owner jingled the coins in his hand. "Ver-ree fun-nee," he said and put the money into a cigar box.

"Other stores would help you wrap it," Bobby pointed out.

The owner took the front page of his racing form and handed it to us. "Here," he said.

It had a big picture of a galloping horse on the top.

"Thanks." Bobby wound the paper around the back scratcher. "She likes horses."

Bobby could find something good about anything or anybody—except Arnie.

Three

The route from the stall to our home led up the steepest hill in Chinatown. Cars always had to shift to low gear. On rainy days, not even that helped.

We were used to hills, but the slope was so steep that it still left us panting. Halfway up my legs began to ache. I puffed to Bobby, "You're moving kind of slow. Maybe we should rest a moment."

Bobby, though, continued to climb. "I'm fine, but if you want to rest, we can." He must be part mountain goat.

"I was just thinking of you," I grumbled, and started after him.

18

Bobby had his book bag in one hand and the back scratcher in the other. "Mom's really going to like this."

"As long as I get my dime's worth," I said.

The hill was so steep that I had to lean forward. So I was busy looking at the sidewalk rather than the top of the hill.

"There you are," a voice shouted from above us.

I looked up to see a man standing on the top of the hill. Or at least I thought it was a man. However, he was wearing a maroon sweater, blue shirt, and corduroy pants. I couldn't figure out what a man would be doing in our school uniform.

He came down toward us, smacking a meaty fist into a palm. "I've been looking all over for you."

I recognized that voice now. It was Arnie-zilla.

"We should've headed straight home." I groaned.

"Yeah." Bobby edged in closer toward me automatically. I wasn't going to be much protection, though.

Arnie stopped about a yard from us, rising and falling on the balls of his feet. He was wearing a big grin on his face. "You ready for a pounding, squirts?"

I set my book bag down. I was ready to meet my fate. Bobby had been leading me toward this massacre ever since he was born.

I put up my fists defiantly. "You and what army?"

His fists looked the size of hams. "I don't need any army."

Suddenly Bobby sprang past me. "You leave him alone." He was waving the back scratcher in the air like a sword.

Arnie's hand shot out. "Who's going to make me? You?"

"Hey!" Bobby said as Arnie snatched the back scratcher out of Bobby's grasp.

Bobby stretched out his hands. "Give that back!"

I got a headlock on Bobby and held him. I wouldn't mind becoming an only child again—but not that way. "Cut it out, Bobby."

"But that's Mother's gift," Bobby protested.

Arnie stiffened and he glared at us. You'd think we'd called him frass head again.

"Aren't you Mama's little babies?" Arnie sneered. He spun around, holding out the back scratcher. As it hit a streetlamp, our gift broke with an ugly snap.

Bobby was so furious that he had to open his mouth again. "You're a mean old frass head."

Arnie wagged the broken stem not at Bobby but at me. "I'm going to make your life so miserable, Teddy."

"He's the one who called you that," I protested. "I'm not even sure what 'frass head' means."

Arnie threw the broken stem away with a laugh. "But you're the one who got me dragged in front of Sister Principal," Arnie said. "I'm going to pound you tomorrow and every day after that."

Well, I guess I knew what my future was going to be: pretty bleak.

"See you tomorrow, Mama's Boy," he said, and took a comb from his back pocket. He began work on his hair as he walked away.

"I hope your gel melts," I muttered to his back.

Bobby came back with our gift cradled in both hands. "It's broken." He sounded almost ready to cry.

I felt like crying, too. I felt like swearing as well. "Don't you have any brains? Why'd you have to make him madder? He would have stopped today with just a couple of black eyes. Now the pounding's going to stretch on."

"He was going to hit you," Bobby said.

I just stared at him. Little brothers. They drag you into a feud with someone who could go ten rounds with King Kong. And yet . . . and yet they try to protect you.

I couldn't stay mad at my pint-size bodyguard. "Maybe I can transfer to another school."

Bobby was picking up the pieces. "Why would he do something like that? I'd never do anything like that to him."

Bobby was smart about a lot of things. He knew all kinds of facts, but he didn't know the first thing about the facts of life.

So I tried to explain things to him. "There are two kinds of people in this world—the bullies and the victims. Guess which bunch we belong to?"

"But why does it have to be that way?" he asked as he tried to fit the pieces together.

Yeah, why? I didn't have any answers, though, so I simply shrugged. "It just is."

"But it's not right," he said.

"No, it isn't." I sighed and waved my hand at him. "Leave the pieces. Let's just get another one."

"I don't have more money," he said. "I spent everything I had on Mom's gift."

I laughed because I thought I had caught him in a lie. "You've got plenty of money. You hardly ever buy anything."

"I gave it to the orphans in the Solomons," Bobby said.

The nuns who ran our school had a mission in the Solomon Islands in the Pacific Ocean.

I sighed. I thought of all the movies I could have seen and all the comic books I could have bought. "You're such a goody-goody."

"But they could get books and shoes—" Bobby began.

"I know. I heard the same lecture from the nuns." I just hadn't let it stick to me like Bobby. He was a regular little saint.

"What do we do for Mom now?" Bobby looked ready to cry.

That's the problem with saints. They aren't good at fixing things like leaky pipes. They have to ask their big brothers instead.

23

"We can fix it," I said.

"How?" Bobby asked doubtfully.

I came up with the first thing that popped into my head. "We'll use a Popsicle stick," I said. "Then we'll wrap Scotch tape around it. That should work."

"It's going to look ugly," Bobby complained.

"Mother won't care. We've tried our best," I said, and added, "Isn't that what she always tells us?"

Bobby brightened. "Yeah."

That was one problem solved. I just wish I could solve Arnie-zilla so easily.

Four

The war started as soon as I got to school. Stairs led down from the street to a passageway that led to the basketball court. Arnie was just like a troll. He was waiting beneath the stairs.

When he saw me, he stepped out of the shadows. "There you are," he said, punching his hand. There was a nasty grin on his face.

"Run, Bobby!" I was already ducking the blow. His fist sounded like the wind. It could have knocked down a tree. Arnie made a strangling sound.

I pounded down the tunnel. Ahead was the sunlight in the court.

"Teddy," Bobby called.

I whirled around. Arnie had Bobby by the collar. My little brother was never very fast. Bobby looked at me desperately.

I did the only thing I could. I threw my history book. It didn't sail like a Frisbee. Its boxy shape made it fly funny. It jerked through the air like a wounded pigeon. I missed Arnie by five feet. It hit the metal steps with a *clong*.

However, it distracted Arnie. Bobby was able to break free. He came racing down the corridor. Arnie came close behind him.

I ran toward Bobby's teacher, Sister Ann. "Sister," I said.

She turned with a smile.

I stopped, panting. "Bobby and Arnie are a little shy. They're having a problem with their math homework. But they're afraid to ask."

Sister Ann looked over my head and raised a hand. "Arnie, Bobby. Come here."

Arnie and Bobby immediately slowed to a walk. As they came toward us, Sister Ann murmured, "Next time Arnie picks on someone, just come to me. No one will think you're a tattletale."

I'd had Sister Ann last year. She was pretty sharp. However, there was still a code in the playground. I was no rat. I could only use this trick once.

I slipped away as they came forward. Arnie glared at me. "Later," he muttered.

I had only delayed the pounding. Miserably I went back to the steps to get my history book. I'd cracked the spine. The book was ruined.

Suddenly it all got to me. I sat down on the steps. Now my teacher was going to be mad at me, too.

"Maybe we can fix it with tape," Bobby said.

I jerked my head up in alarm. "Where's Arnie?"

Bobby grinned. "Sister's still got him. She's going over his math homework with him."

I didn't see why the little weasel should be happy. First, he'd started the feud with Arnie. Now he'd used up my best excuse. I'd been stupid to get involved.

I cradled the pieces of my book as I got up. "You're dumb and you're slow. And you pick fights with the wrong people. You keep dragging me into messes and then expect me to clean them up.

You're not a brother. You're a stone around my neck."

"I don't mean to be so much trouble, Teddy."

I pushed him out of the way. "Just leave me alone."

I got a scolding for my carelessness with my history book, but my teacher had this great tape. It would probably hold my book together for the year. And next year the school was adopting new books.

All the rest of the day I dodged Arnie. Most of the time I stayed glued to a nun. When I couldn't find a nun, I ducked into the chapel. Even Arnie would not hit anyone there.

In the cool, shadowy chapel, I sat and tried to figure a way out. I couldn't outmuscle Arnie. My friends were all cowards, so I couldn't outnumber him. I didn't have enough money to bribe him.

I was a dead man.

Five

I was still hunting for an answer when I went to my Chinese lesson. Our school had an hour of Chinese during the daytime. Students from several classes were grouped by ability, not by age, so Bobby was in my intermediate class, too.

We were taught by Miss Lee. She liked to wear Chinese-style dresses that had a slit up one leg. She liked the old-fashioned Chinese discipline, too. Put a ruler into her hand, and I'd match her against any marine.

At any rate, today Miss Lee announced in Chinese that we would have guests today. "Mr.

Chin is sick, so his advanced class will sit with us. It means things will be crowded."

When the other students filed in, I was surprised to see Arnie among them. I figured someone had made a big mistake if they had put him in the advanced class.

The others from the advanced class began to sit on the floor or wherever they could. However, Arnie went over to Ollie and glared.

Ollie slid out of his seat quickly. "You look tired. Have a seat." And he scuttled over to a corner safely out of reach.

As the lesson started, I tried to shrink behind my desk so she wouldn't notice me. However, Miss Lee could smell fear. She always found me.

When Miss Lee asked me a question on an emperor, I used my favorite Chinese phrase. "I don't know."

"You're so stupid," Miss Lee said. Fortunately she had left her ruler on the desk. She used it to hit you when you made too many mistakes. "Don't you ever study?"

I always had trouble with our Chinese lessons. When I learned something new, it always drove out something old.

Miss Lee turned slowly. Everywhere heads bobbed down as students tried to avoid eye contact. Only Arnie returned her stare.

"Do you know what dynasty he was in?" she asked Arnie.

To everyone's amazement, he said, "He was in the Ming dynasty." It was the only time I saw him smile without making someone else cry.

As Miss Lee went through the lesson, Arnie was the only one who knew all the answers. He'd gone from being the dummy in the American classes to being the star in the Chinese class. And he liked it. Most of the time he slouched; but in Chinese class he sat up straight.

Finally Miss Lee focused her sights on me again. "Write the word for *lightning* on the board."

I longed to stay put, but I didn't want to be demoted. I might wind up with the slow class. I dragged my feet up to the blackboard. When I tried to write the Chinese character, everyone laughed.

Arnie was the only one who didn't. "You're missing a stroke," he whispered.

I turned in surprise. He held up a sheet of paper with the word. I saw my mistake.

"Thanks," I whispered gratefully as I headed back to my seat.

Suddenly I went flying through the air. Everyone laughed again when I landed. As I sat up, Arnie drew his foot in.

"Later," he grinned wickedly. Arnie-zilla was back.

When class ended, Bobby stopped by my desk. "Arnie helped you," he said.

"Just to set me up for tripping me," I grumbled.

"I think he did that to save his reputation," Bobby said. "I mean, everyone saw him do something nice, so he figured he had to do something bad." He looked thoughtful.

Every time Bobby had an idea it meant trouble for me. "A pounding's a pounding."

"But how would you feel if you were smart but everyone treated you like a dummy?" Bobby asked. "Wouldn't you get mad, too?"

"Arnie was born mad," I said, rubbing my forehead. I was already starting to get a headache.

Bobby snapped his fingers. "I bet if we tried to see his point of view, we might be able to set up a truce."

For one moment, Arnie had stopped being Arnie-zilla. Maybe there was hope. Then I shook it off. Bobby always looked at the world through rose-colored glasses.

"The world doesn't work that way," I said. "Let's just get out of school right away."

However, when the final bell rang, I couldn't find any sign of my brother.

I got an itchy feeling inside. My little brother was going to get into an even worse mess.

Well, so what? All my life I'd been giving in to Bobby. I'd had to share everything with him—my bedroom, my toys, my books. And it wasn't because I liked him. It was only because he was my brother.

I had every right to get out of this situation on my own. What Bobby did was his problem. Unfortunately, old habits die hard.

I grabbed one of the kids in Bobby's class. "Have you seen my brother?"

The kid shook his head. "He was looking for Arnie."

"But you guys are in the same class," I said.

"I know, but Sister took Arnie to Sister Principal's

office about something," the kid said. "Bobby went after him. He said he had business with him."

"Yeah, hospital business," I said, and hurried away.

I walked against the flow of students, looking for Bobby.

Suddenly Bobby came around the corner. "Come on. Let's go," I said, grabbing his arm.

"I've got to find Arnie," he said, pulling free.

"He'll stuff you into the nearest garbage can," I warned.

Bobby shrugged. "I figured I couldn't make a peace treaty without getting a few punches first."

"Let's just get out of here," I said. I tried to grab him again, but a sudden flow of students cut me off.

He gave me a brave little smile. "You go on home. Don't worry about me."

"Bobby," I called. "Come back."

I saw his head bobbing as it disappeared toward the rear of the school. I tried to follow, but I got bumped so much that I felt like a fish swimming against the current.

When the flow of students finally slowed to a

trickle, I headed for the stairs leading down to the school yard. I took them two at a time.

Arnie had Bobby by the rear gate to the school yard. He towered over the garbage cans there like Godzilla over Tokyo Bay.

"I thought you'd try to sneak out. Chicken," he sneered.

"I was looking for you," Bobby said.

"Sure you were." He made clucking noises.

"We've got to talk," Bobby said. "I wanted to thank you for helping my brother today."

That only made Arnie madder. "You figured that I was getting soft, didn't you? Well, I'll show you." Arnie raised a fist as big as a softball. Bobby squeezed his eyes shut, waiting for the blows.

"Pick on someone your own size," I said.

Arnie jerked his head at me. "I'll take care of you later, Teddy."

"You don't want to hit the shrimp," I said. "Take my word on it. He doesn't bounce well. I've tried it."

"Okay, if you want to take his place." He dropped Bobby and whirled around. Leaning over the top of a can, he started to swing his fist forward.

I have to admit it. I shut my eyes and waited for the pain. When it didn't come, I peeked.

Arnie's mouth and nose were wrinkled with disgust. His fist still hovered in the air. At first, I thought he'd got hit by some kind of superfreeze ray. But then he said, "Ugh."

I seized my chance. "I don't want any trouble, Arnie."

When he just kept staring, I tried to join him on the same side of the cans. "I'm glad to see you're being reasonable."

Arnie actually took a step back. "Stay away from me."

"What are you scared of?" I asked, spreading my hands.

Arnie jabbed his finger at me. "There's a bug on you, stupid."

I looked down. A cockroach had crawled onto my shirt. "Ugh," I said. I raised my hands to brush it off. However, that meant touching it. "Ugh," I repeated. My face must have looked as disgusted as Arnie's. I was just as frozen. I was afraid of making the cockroach move any higher or lower.

"Gosh, Arnie," Bobby said in a sweet voice.

"Don't tell me you're scared of a little-bitty cock-roach?"

"They're awful," Arnie said petrified.

"I bet he's more scared of you," Bobby said. He turned to me. "May I?"

I swallowed. "Help yourself."

Bobby cupped one hand like a platform against my stomach. He raised his free hand slowly. "It's hard to sneak up on cockroaches from the rear. They have these two little hairs back there. They feel any change in the air—like a hand coming down."

I was tired of being treated like a human guinea pig. "Hurry up, Bobby," I said through clenched teeth.

"Come on, now," Bobby coaxed the cockroach. He slowly lowered his hand toward the rear of the cockroach. Sure enough the cockroach surged forward onto the palm of his other hand.

"You're letting that dirty bug touch you." Arnie's voice went very high.

Cupping his hand, Bobby started to stretch it toward Arnie. "He's not dirty. Cockroaches are as fussy as cats. They're always grooming themselves."

It was funny how Bobby knew everything about science and nothing about baseball.

Arnie lifted his arms to protect himself. "Get away from me," he said.

"Cockroaches don't have noses, either," Bobby said, staring at the bug in fascination. "They breathe through the openings on their belly and they smell through their antennae. See how they're wriggling toward you. It's sniffing you now."

Arnie started to back up before my little brother. I wished I had a camera.

"And did you know that cockroaches have two brains?" Bobby asked, pursuing him.

The faster Arnie retreated, the faster Bobby followed. All the time he spouted more facts about the cockroach until Arnie broke and ran.

"Did you know that a female cockroach can lay up to forty eggs at one time. And do that eight times?" Bobby shouted after him. Arnie picked up speed. "And in just five months?"

When he was gone, Bobby turned around and grinned in triumph. "I didn't think so."

Six

Long after Arnie was gone, Bobby gazed down at the cockroach in his hand.

It gave me the creeps watching that roach crawl around. He was getting covered with cockroach cooties. "Get rid of that disgusting thing," I said.

"Bugs are almost as interesting as alligators," Bobby said, studying it.

"Cockroaches eat garbage," I said.

"We throw away all this perfectly good food. Then we get mad when someone else wants to use it." He shrugged. "Just because something's different doesn't make it a monster."

Leave it to Bobby to make me feel guilty for hating bugs. "That's true about humans, but cockroaches are a whole different species," I said, keeping my distance from my strange little brother.

Bobby held out the cockroach toward me. I was afraid he was going to chase me around like he had Arnie. "He wouldn't seem so disgusting if you looked at things from his view. I mean, we're weird to him. We've only got two legs and we wear our skeletons on the inside."

"Well, where's his skeleton?" I asked, curious despite my disgust.

Bobby moved the finger of his free hand in an arc. "On the outside. It's like armor around all his squishy parts. If you think about it, it makes more sense that way. He protects all his important soft stuff. But we have all our padding around our bones. And yet they're the hardest thing inside us."

As Bobby talked, I felt a little dizzy. Bobby made me feel as if I had suddenly stood upside down on my head.

First, Bobby had been the one to save me. Now he was asking me to look at things through a bug's eyes.

"Just get rid of it, will you?" I grumbled.

Bobby drew his eyebrows together. "What if Arnie ambushes us on the way home?" He held up the cockroach. "He's like our own miniature tank."

I wanted to flatten that awful bug, but Bobby had a point. "Okay, but dump him when we get home."

"And what will we do tomorrow?" Bobby asked. "And the day after tomorrow?"

Arnie or cockroach cooties—two great choices. I threw up my hands. "Okay, okay. I guess we'll have to keep him for a while. With a little luck, Arnie will get mad at someone else and forget all about us." I added. "And wash your hands before you touch anything at home."

Bobby carefully stowed him in his shirt pocket. "Now, you stay there, little fellow," he cooed to it.

I made a note to myself. Washing his hands wouldn't be enough now. I'd make sure that Bobby took a whole bath. And all his clothes were going to be washed in hot water. Maybe that would get rid of all the cockroach cooties.

Bobby had his Chinese ink box. It was a small metal box about the size of a lady's compact.

Engraved on the lid was a picture of a carp becoming a dragon. In it was a small ball of cotton soaked in Chinese ink. Chinese ink was thicker and blacker than American ink. You could add water to the cotton. Then you'd have enough ink for the handwriting lessons.

He dumped the cotton into a garbage can and cleaned the ink box with a tissue. Then he eased his hand into his shirt pocket. "Good boy," he beamed at the cockroach. He held his hand over the box so that it crawled inside.

"Now we'd better find out how to care for our protector," Bobby said. "In fact, maybe we should get another cockroach. That way we can each have one." He started to examine the garbage cans.

I held up my hands. "No thanks. I'll just stay close to you." I waved him away as he got too near. "But not too close." Two yards seemed like a good distance. Then he'd be close enough to come to the rescue. At the same time all those cockroach cooties were far enough away—I hoped.

As we left the school, I checked for Arnie. However, there wasn't any sign of him. "The coast is clear." I sighed.

"I'm ready for him," Bobby said, bumping into me.

I waved him away from me. "Two paces back."

"I don't mind, but you're going to hurt Hercules' feelings," Bobby said.

"Hercules?" I asked.

"He'll protect us. So that's a good name for him." Bobby held up the box. "Don't you think so, Hercules?"

It was bad enough my life depended on a bug. I didn't want to get on a first-name basis with it, too. "It's just a bug."

"Why don't people like bugs?" Bobby asked.

I gave a snort. "That's pretty obvious. They're ugly."

"But some bugs are beautiful," Bobby said. Sometimes my little brother was beyond embarrassing.

"Well, sure, maybe butterflies," I admitted, "but I could squish the rest."

"But some bugs have wings like rainbows that are just as pretty," Bobby argued. "And their bodies can come in all different colors. Bright reds and silvery blues. Like someone squeezed out tubes of paint."

I should have known better than to argue with

the human encyclopedia of weirdness. "But Hercules is just a cockroach."

That puzzled Bobby. "But you like to read fantasy books with lots of magic, right?"

"So what?" I asked suspiciously.

"Well, nature's as good as any fantasy book. It's full of stuff that's just like magic." He smiled proudly at the cockroach. "Hercules is like a warrior from one of your fantasy books."

"You'll never get me to read his story." I smirked.

"Hercules may look small, but he's tougher than us. Cockroaches live everywhere in the world—even at the North and South Poles. If you dropped an atom bomb on San Francisco, Hercules would still survive. He could even live a week without his head," Bobby said excitedly. "I'd like to see a knight or wizard that tough."

Even though I thought I might get nightmares tonight, I was beginning to feel a little of his excitement. "So every night is an adventure."

"Hercules enters the sunless kingdom of the giants," Bobby said, his eyes shining. "He searches for the treasure in his armor."

44

Never mind that the treasure might be some rotten meat. Bobby had appealed to my imagination. "And the armor is enchanted. It lets him sense things from behind," I said.

"And all around, despite the dark," Bobby agreed.

Bobby had managed to turn things upside down once again. It was strange to see his point of view . . . and yet it was kind of fun, too. I mean, the whole world was one big fantasy adventure to him.

"I guess we'll take the bug along." It felt odd agreeing with him. "But don't lift the lid if you can help it," I warned. "I don't want that bug—"

Bobby started to frown.

I corrected myself quickly. "I mean, Hercules, getting loose." Something had been bugging—I mean, bothering me, too. I turned around and backed up the hill. "Why did you go looking for Arnie? That was dumb. You should have left with me."

"I got you into this," Bobby said. "Now I'm going to get you out. I don't mean to be a stone around your neck."

Me and my big mouth. That was the problem

with Bobby. Just when I had worked up a good grudge, he did something like this to make me feel guilty. At times like these, I even liked him better than I liked myself.

The Chinatown streets were filled with people shopping for their dinners. There were always plenty of fresh vegetables and meat and fish and fruit. Everyone had bulging plastic shopping bags. We wound our way through the crowd. If they only knew about Hercules, we would have a clear path.

As we started to climb the hills, the sidewalks started to clear. However, the streets were full of cars grumbling as they climbed the steep slope. At the intersection above, I saw a cable car rattle by. It was full of shivering tourists in T-shirts and shorts.

"Do you think Mama will let me keep Hercules as a pet?" Bobby asked.

After Oscar, our alligator, we'd had a turtle for a little while. It hadn't lasted long, though, much to Bobby's sorrow.

Hercules was probably as much pet as we'd be allowed nowadays. Even if we managed to work things out with Arnie somehow, maybe we'd still keep the bug. I liked the idea of having a little magic around—as weird and creepy as it might be.

I shrugged. "As long as you don't tell her, I guess you can."

Seven

When we got to our apartment house, Bobby headed next door.

"Where are you going?" I asked. "We've got to get ready for the banquet."

"We need to know about how to take care of Hercules," Bobby argued. He pointed at the windows where all sorts of dead spiders and beetles were decorations. "The Bug Lady can tell us what to do."

The bug decorations had first appeared around Halloween time, so the neighborhood had thought she was decorating for the holidays. However, they

48

stayed up through Christmas. (The bigger ones had reindeer antlers made out of pieces of pipe cleaners. At Easter they had bunny ears.) To everyone's horror except Bobby's, we realized the bugs were some kind of statement.

Our landlord, Mr. Wong, had complained. The Bug Lady, though, was the daughter of the man who owned the apartment house next door. The real estate agent, who handled the property, explained, "Her father is just glad to have her out of his own house."

"But what does that weird woman do?" Mr. Wong asked.

"She's a graduate student at Berkeley in entomology," the agent said.

"What's that?" Mr. Wong asked.

"She studies bugs," the agent said, and pointed at the windows. "All those things are her homework."

When Mr. Wong had told my family, we all thought the Bug Lady was kind of creepy. Only Bobby had thought she was cool.

I didn't even want to go up the steps, but Bobby went right to the doorbell and rang it.

When there wasn't any answer, he tried again. When no one came to the door, I felt relieved. "I guess the Bug Lady isn't home."

"Just wait," Bobby said and rang a third time. "Sometimes she's so busy with her insects, she doesn't notice the doorbell right away."

"How do you know?" I asked.

"How do you think I earned my money for Mama's present?" Bobby said.

"You went in there?" I asked. "Does Mama know about it?"

"Of course not. I wanted the present to be a surprise," Bobby said. "I got permission from Papa. He told me I could, but I had to wash my hands."

I had noticed that Bobby had been unusually clean lately. "Just what were you doing?" I asked suspiciously.

"Cleaning out the cages," Bobby said. "That's when I learned about frass."

I wouldn't have made Bobby just wash his hands. I would have hosed him down. I edged another yard away from him.

Finally I heard a thumping on the stairs. Someone was coming.

I started to get a little scared, but Bobby was calm. I couldn't be more scared than Bobby.

When the door opened, I had been expecting a mad scientist in a lab coat, with crazy hair. However, the Bug Lady was in a sweatshirt and jeans. She looked perfectly normal. In fact, except for her bare feet, she looked like she could sell insurance.

"Bobby," she said with a smile. "It's not the day to clean the cages."

"Hello, Charlie," Bobby said. "We've come to ask for some advice. This is Hercules," he added, opening the ink box. Hercules waved his antennae. Apparently, Bobby was introducing us in order of importance.

Charlie leaned so close that Hercules could have crawled up her nose. "Ah, a fine specimen of *Periplaneta americana*. It actually started off in Africa, but its ancestors migrated here several centuries ago."

"How?" I asked.

"Probably stowed away in the holds of ships," Charlie said.

"And this is my big brother, Teddy," Bobby said, nodding to me.

51

"And a fine specimen of *Homo sapiens*," Charlie said and stuck out her hand. "Pleased to meet you. My name's Charlotte, but everyone calls me Charlie."

My skin felt like crawling off my bones. I touched just her fingertips and raised and lowered my hand once out of politeness. Then I jerked my hand away.

"Teddy," Bobby said, embarrassed.

However, Charlie didn't seem insulted at all. I think she was used to people doing that. "So are you a budding scientist, too?"

I opened my mouth to answer, but the words froze on my lips. All I could do was stare. At first, I thought it was a black pipe cleaner on her shoulder. Then it wriggled and I realized it was a leg. And the leg was attached to a fuzzy body. A large fuzzy body the size of my fist.

Charlie was puzzled by my silence. "Or maybe you're interested in something besides science," she said uncertainly.

All I could do was stare as the biggest spider I had ever seen crawled up Charlie's back and onto her shoulder. It began to move toward her neck.

I had stumbled into the middle of a horror movie. "Hold still, and I'll get it!" I lifted my book bag.

Bobby grabbed my wrists. "No, that's Madeline!"

The Bug Lady twisted her head to look at her shoulder. "So that's where you went to." She put up her hand and calmly let that monster move onto her palm. "Madeline likes to play hide-and-seek." Who knew if Madeline had even bigger cousins up there. Maybe there were spiders the size of footballs.

I said to Bobby, "You talk to Charlie, Bobby. I just remembered I got important things to do at home."

"Madeline will be so disappointed," Charlie said. "She loves company so."

I bet. Especially if the company was tied up in a spiderweb.

"Say hello, Madeline," Charlie urged.

I would have sworn that Madeline waved a hairy leg at me. I tried to return the hello. However, I was so scared my throat tightened up. All I could make were croaking sounds.

"Now, don't be scared of Madeline," Charlie said, cradling the spider in front of her. "She wouldn't harm a fly. Well, that's not true. Flies are in danger, but you and I are not. Well, that's not true, either. Madeline bit me when we first met, but we've been buddies ever since."

"You mean she's a pet?" I asked, edging back another a step.

"No, more of a colleague. Well, that's not true. She's the coauthor of my dissertation." Charlie chuckled. "My life story as told by Madeline." She nodded up at the window. "And those were some of the other coauthors."

If I had to write about anything, I would write about sports, not bugs. "Did she kill some of them?"

"Well, she is a tarantula," Charlie said. "So now, to what do we owe the pleasure of your visit?"

"We want to know how to care for Hercules," Bobby piped up. He held up the box for a closer look.

Charlie turned sideways so that Madeline was away from the box. "Don't let her get near Hercules, or we could have an unfortunate accident."

Bobby closed the lid on the box. "Can you help us?"

"Sure, let's check my books," Charlie said. She stepped to the side. "After you."

I would have left for home at that point, but that little weasel hipped me. "You first," Bobby said as I stumbled inside the bug house.

Eight

"I'm afraid I use the steps as a second library," Charlie apologized. There were stacks of books and papers on each step. It left only a narrow lane in between the stacks. Our mother would have had a fit.

"Just follow me and don't touch anything," Charlie warned. I didn't need to be told, though. Who knows what bugs were hiding in the piles?

That made for problems. What if there were bugs on the ceiling? They might drop down on me. I kept looking from step to ceiling. Several times Bobby bumped into me.

The hallway was even worse. There were book-cases on either side, so the aisle was even narrower. As I walked along, I heard a scuttling sound. Turning, I saw a spider even larger than Madeline inside a glass tank. Its body was as large as a lemon, and it was covered all over with fur like a stuffed doll. It tapped at the window of the tank. I think it wanted out.

Charlie mistook my horrified stare. "That's Arthur. He comes from British Guiana. I thought he'd love the hallway. I've heard that children in his native country keep them as pets and lead them around on strings."

I pivoted slowly. I realized that all the bookcases held cages filled with spiders as well as books. This was worse than a horror movie. It was a nightmare.

"Come on, Teddy." The little weasel pushed me from behind.

I was so scared that I couldn't think. My legs moved automatically like a zombie's.

Ahead, I could hear a loud chirping that sounded like a huge cricket.

Charlie paused by a doorway and motioned us inside. "Enter."

I would have sworn Madeline also waved a bristly leg. I hesitated on the threshold, but I didn't see any monster bug.

It looked like many living rooms in San Francisco. There was a fireplace against one wall. Cabinets with glass doors stood on either side. Bright light poured through the bay windows. It made the dead insects look like black paper cutouts. There were even regular chairs to sit on instead of spiderwebs.

The chirping came from one of the cabinets. Bobby crossed to it and squatted down. "Hey, fellows. How are you doing?"

The cabinet was filled with crickets. They hopped around cheerfully. At least I liked their looks better than the spider's. "You write about them, too?"

"No, they're snacks for some of our friends." Charlie gestured toward the spiders in the hallway.

"But they look so happy," I said. It didn't seem right to feed them to those monsters.

"You can't go to the supermarket and buy a bag of dried spider chow," Bobby said. "They eat live things."

Charlie saw the expression on my face. "Don't look like that, Teddy. Spiders have a lot of human virtues. They're brave, hardy and resourceful. They're loving, too."

"Loving?" I asked skeptically.

"Spiders can be loving mothers," Charlie said. "They'll fight to protect their young. And some of them are true artists and architects when it comes to weaving their webs. Their webs are amazing— ounce for ounce that lace can be stronger than steel."

I looked around at some of the jars on one shelf. They were filled with spiderwebs. "Spiderwebs?"

"If you could make steel as thin as a web strand, the strand would be stronger," Charlie explained. "The webs are even strong enough to let them fly."

Bobby swiveled around. "Really?"

Charlie arched her fingers like an overturned bowl. "The young of some spiders weave these little parachutes when it's time to leave their mother. Then the wind catches their parachutes and carries them away."

Bobby started to get excited. "Do you have any?"

"No, but I've seen them on field trips," Charlie said.

"I didn't know bugs could do that," I confessed.

Charlie smiled patiently. "Spiders aren't bugs."

She and Bobby began to discuss spider stuff happily. It was like Ollie and me talking about football.

As she chatted, Charlie cleared a bunch of large jars off the chairs and set them on the floor. "Take a load off your feet, Teddy," she urged.

My legs were feeling pretty shaky by now. "Thanks."

As I eased into the chair, Charlie stacked the jars behind me. Suddenly she held up one of the jars at shoulder height. "Look, Madeline. Cynthia's babies are hatching."

There was a fuzzy ball inside a jar. From it, little black dots began to spill out. They were about the size of a pinhead.

"Finally." Bobby ran over. "Look, Teddy!" He always wanted to share his happiness with me. Sometimes, though, I wished he kept it to himself.

It was funny, but I felt so out of place here. This

was Bobby's turf. Just like Chinese school was Arnie's.

Charlie helpfully showed me the jar. Inside were a gazillion tiny spiders. With a new, horrified thought, I looked at all the jars Charlie had taken from the chair and put on the floor. They were filled with other fuzzy balls, too—each of them with a different mama spider. The chair was a spider nursery.

I jumped up so fast I nearly knocked the jar out of Charlie's hands. "Careful," she said. Worried, she backed up.

Embarrassed, I massaged the back of my leg. "I got a charley horse." I stamped my foot a couple of times. "But it's all gone."

Before I sat down again, though, I checked out the chair. There were no little black dots scampering around on it. Even so, once I sat down, I thought I could feel thousands of tiny little feet crawling over me.

As Charlie and Bobby chatted merrily about Cynthia's children, I tried to get a hold of myself.

Calm down, Arnie is still worse than spiders, I told myself. However, I wasn't quite so certain anymore.

When I heard the hissing, at first I thought it was the steam radiator. However, I didn't know of any radiators at ankle height. And the hissing moved from my left to my right.

I sat frozen, torn between curiosity and fear.

Curiosity won out. I looked down. By my foot was the biggest cockroach I had ever seen. It reared up on its forelegs and hissed like a teakettle with six legs.

People six blocks away must have heard my scream. In a panic, I jumped up on the seat of the chair. However, the chair wasn't that steady.

To my horror, I felt the chair tipping. I waved my arms for balance, but that was no good. The chair banged against the floor.

Stunned, I lay on my back. That's when I saw eyes, lots of little beady bug eyes. They were staring back at me.

There were more of them above me in the pyramid of jars. Big bugs. Little bugs. Green bugs. Blue bugs. Thin bugs. Fat bugs. And all of them just watching me like I was the biggest meal they had ever seen.

"Ack!" I shouted, as I tried to scramble to my feet.

Bobby could talk all he wanted about Hercules' point of view. I never want to be at eye level with a bug again.

However, Charlie was too busy with my discovery. Stooping, she had put her hand on the floor. "Oh, there you are, Sidney. So that's where you'd gotten to. You naughty boy. You had me worried." And the biggest cockroach I ever saw crawled onto her palm. From the bug's smell, it could have used deodorant.

I understood why her parents kicked Charlie out of their house. Then I had the scariest thought of all. Would Bobby be the same way when he grew up? I didn't want to stick around to find out.

In the meantime, Bobby was busy introducing Hercules to Sidney. "Hercules, meet your big cousin, Sidney. He's from Madagascar."

I wondered what else had gotten loose in Charlie's apartment. There could be a lot worse things than cockroach cooties. When I got home, I wanted to take a bath and wash all my clothes.

In the meantime, Sidney was resting on Charlie's palm.

Bobby had opened the lid to the ink box again

so Hercules could peer out. "You and Sidney are going to be good friends."

Charlie put Sidney into another aquarium tank. "Now, you stay there this time. Eat your banana," she scolded. Then she turned to me. "I don't know how to thank you for helping me find Sidney."

"Just help us with Hercules," I said, wanting to get out of there.

Charlie smiled oddly. "I can do better than that. Won't you have tea with me and Madeline?"

My stomach started to growl. "A snack might be nice," I admitted.

"Will you give me a hand, Bobby?" Charlie asked.

"Sure," Bobby said, shutting the lid on Hercules. He came over and set the ink box by my feet. "Keep Teddy company," he said to the cockroach, and then he whispered to me. "Drink what you like, but don't eat anything."

"Why?" I said, startled.

However, Bobby was already following Charlie through the swinging door into the kitchen.

What was that warning about? Then I remembered Sidney and Madeline on Charlie's hands. I wouldn't want to eat food that had been handled by her buggy hands.

When I heard running water, though, I tiptoed across the floor and peeked through the door. Charlie and Bobby were both washing their hands. The warning hadn't been necessary after all.

I skirted around Hercules and righted the chair. Then I checked for bugs, and the chair looked clean so I sat down. I felt thousands of eyes watching me.

With Madeline still perched on his shoulder, Charlie came back with a huge tray. She paused uncertainly in the living room, looking for clear space. "Clear those wolf spiders from the table, will you, Bobby?"

Bobby calmly set the jars on the floor. Then Charlie set down a platter of cookies of all different types. "You're in luck, Teddy. I just baked these myself."

They certainly looked tempting. As she poured tea, Charlie instructed Bobby in the care and feeding of cockroaches. I just tuned them out. I didn't want to lose my appetite. Besides, the chocolate chip cookies smelled especially good.

"Help yourself, Teddy," Charlie urged, holding

out a plate to me. Eagerly I took it and piled the plate high. I figured Bobby had just been trying to scare me off. That way he'd have the cookies all to himself when he visited Charlie.

"My, you've got quite an appetite." Charlie laughed.

"I'm a growing boy," I said, still avoiding looking at Madeline.

"Well, take more," she coaxed.

I wasn't going to be shy. I scooped up another six chocolate chip cookies.

It was only then that I saw Bobby shake his head. I didn't see what the problem was, though. Charlie had washed her hands.

"Won't you help yourself?" Charlie asked, and held out a plate to my little brother.

"Thanks," Bobby said. When it came to sweets, Bobby could be a human vacuum cleaner. I'd seen him once go through a whole bag of Oreos by himself. However, this time, he only took a couple of the smallest cookies.

"Take more," Charlie insisted.

"No, I . . . I already ate before I came here," Bobby fibbed.

I looked back at the cookies. They seemed fine.

I watched Charlie closely. She took a couple of cookies and began to munch away happily. "Hmm, I love these."

I picked up a chocolate chip cookie. It was just about to go into my mouth, when Bobby coughed loudly. I glanced at him. He shook his head again. Charlie was happily chowing down. I still couldn't see what the problem was.

With a shrug, I began to raise the cookie to my mouth again.

Suddenly the clock over the mantel chimed. Bobby jumped to his feet. "We've lost track of the time. We've got Mom's birthday party."

I looked at the clock. "We're going to be late. Dad's going to be mad."

Bobby turned to Charlie and Madeline. "Thanks for all the tips," he said.

Charlie wiped her mouth with a napkin and swallowed a last mouthful of cookie. "Feel free to come over or call anytime."

While Bobby's back was turned, I slipped the chocolate chip cookies into my jacket pocket. I could always eat them later when he wasn't watching. The beauty of it was that I wouldn't have to share my treats like I usually did.

Charlie winked at me. Madeline waved good-bye.

Nine

We raced out of the Bug House and up to our apartment. I fumbled at the lock with my key. Father must have been listening for us. He hated to be late. Our family was always early, even though all our uncles and aunts and cousins were never on time. They would probably stroll in an hour late.

He jerked the door open. "Where have you been? You're late." He pointed at his watch. "We should have been at the restaurant by now."

Mother came up behind him and patted him on the shoulder. "Don't get upset, dear. No one else will be there."

Father tapped his watch. "I'm trying to set an example for the boys. They should use American time, not Chinese time."

Mother pulled Father gently back from the door. "They know, dear."

"I got to clean up," I said, dumping my book bag by the door. I wanted a full bath in hot water. And then disinfectant.

Father caught me by the shoulder. "There's no time for that."

"At least let us change," I protested, entering our apartment.

"No time for that, either," Father said.

I dropped my book bag by the couch while Bobby threw his book bag into a corner. Then Father shepherded us back down the steps and down the hill to Chinatown. By that time, the stores were shutting up tight. Corrugated iron doors covered the fronts and barred grilles guarded the doorways. It was like entering a fort.

"Hurry, hurry," Father kept urging.

Streetcars rattled by. Their antennae crackled on the electrical power lines overhead. Through the windows, we could see commuters and shoppers jammed together like sardines. The buses were like big tin cans on wheels.

We got to the restaurant so early that they still had not turned on the neon sign overhead with the huge pink-and-green dragon. Even so, the restaurant was already crowded. It was a very popular place.

The owner smiled nervously as Father stormed through the door.

"Good evening, sir. We've been waiting for you," he said.

Father was surprised. "For us?"

From somewhere in the restaurant, I heard the sound of splashing. I figured it was the tank that held fresh fish. Maybe they were cleaning it out.

The owner started up the stairs to the banquet room. "Yes. Everyone was here a half hour early." We ate here often. He knew Father's habits well.

"That's impossible," Father said.

"That's what I thought," the owner said. He knew our family's habits, too.

As I climbed the final step, I saw what was making the noise. A stream of water was pouring from the ceiling into a bucket. There were several full

71

buckets on the floor, and a line of empty buckets waiting to be filled. The leaky pipe was right next our family's table.

Father stopped and stared. "What's this?"

"It's water. When's the last time you took a bath?" Uncle Curtis called from a nearby table. He liked teasing Father.

Father stood just out of splashing range. He gazed at it, annoyed. "I know what it is," Father snapped. "I just want to know what it's doing here."

The owner's head bobbed anxiously. "Just a little accident, sir," he said. "The plumber is coming tomorrow."

"Well, that's not going to do us a lot of good tonight." Father frowned. Don't you have any other tables?"

The owner clapped his hands together apologetically. "I'm sorry, sir. We're very crowded."

Father folded his arms. "Then maybe we ought to take our business elsewhere."

For a moment, I thought he was going to make us all tramp over to another restaurant. "But the food's so good here," I protested.

"I wanted this to be a special evening," Father explained in frustration.

"It's all right, dear," Mother said to Father. "I think the water makes things"—she hunted for the right word—"unh . . . festive."

Father scratched his forehead. "I don't see what's festive about a broken pipe."

Mother nudged Father. "Remember when we used to walk by Strawberry Lake in the park?"

Father smiled slowly as he recalled those times. "Oh, yeah. The waterfall."

The owner hovered at Father's elbow. "Yes, sir. You see. We arranged the romantic scene just for you. No extra charge."

"We should go back there sometime," Father said to Mother.

"Can we go to the carousel afterwards?" Bobby piped up.

I didn't care about the carousel. "Can we have pink popcorn?" I knew what counted.

Father rolled his eyes and then grunted. "We're going by ourselves. That's the whole point."

Mother squeezed his arm. "Now, dear. You don't want to disappoint the boys."

"Good-bye, romance," Father grumbled.

"You're too old for that now anyway," Uncle Mat boomed across the big room.

Everyone was there. Uncle Mat's wife, Aunt Martha, and their daughter, Alice, were at one table with Aunt Ethel and Uncle Curtis and their daughter, Nancy. The rest of our relatives, including Cousin Roderick, were at the other tables with Grandmother. Mother's presents lay heaped in a corner.

"Hey, slug, what kept you?" Auntie Ethel called.

Father shook his head. "What are you all doing here?"

"You're always complaining about us being late," Auntie Martha said. "So we thought we'd give you a present, too. We all decided to be early."

"I was the first here," Grandmother proudly announced. She was sitting at another table with some of her Chinatown friends.

"For a change, you were the one who was late." Uncle Curtis wagged a finger at Father. "And for your own wife's party. Shame on you."

"I was ready. It was the boys," Father protested. "They made us late."

Grandmother came to our rescue. "Better late than never," she said, and then got up. She looked at the column of water. "That broken pipe." She sighed in exasperation. She would have to maneuver around it.

Uncle Mat got up with a grin. "I guess it's my turn to ride shotgun."

Grandmother kissed us as she passed. "I'll be back," she promised.

Grandmother could walk on level floors just fine. However, she had a harder time going down the stairs. Uncle Mat took her elbow at the top of the staircase and helped her downstairs to the rest room.

The owner escorted us to the vacant seats.

Uncle Curtis waited until Father sat down. Then he cupped his hands around his mouth. "Bucket time," he shouted and pointed cheerfully at Father.

Ten

The others took up the cry. "Bucket time, bucket time."

Father kept planted in his seat. "I've heard of American time and Chinese time but never bucket time."

Uncle Curtis waved a hand at the bucket. "It's nearly full. Time to put another empty one under there."

"I'll take care of that, sir, this time," the owner promised.

Picking up an empty bucket, he held it underneath the waterfall. At the same time, his foot nudged the brimming bucket to the side. Then he set down the new bucket in its place. He did the whole operation very smoothly. He seemed to have had a lot of practice at it. I wondered how often the pipes broke in his restaurant.

Grandmother came back behind a string of waiters. As she followed them, she sniffed the air. "That winter melon soup smells so good. I can't wait."

Each waiter set a bowl of soup down at a table and began to spoon it out.

"Take away some of those full buckets when you leave," Father told him.

Father should have known better. You just didn't say things like that to a Chinatown waiter. It was like ordering around the president.

The waiter frowned at Father. For a moment, I thought he was going to hit Father with the soup ladle. "It's not my job," he muttered.

Father glared at him. "Well, I'm a customer. It's not my job, either."

The waiter simply ignored Father. He went on serving the soup.

"See if I give you a tip," Father muttered as the

waiters left. However, he waited until the waiter was out of hearing distance.

The soup was as good as it always was. "We could have had something fancier like sharks' fin soup, but we always used to have this. Remember?" Father asked Mother.

Mother smiled over her spoon. "I remember."

With the soup, the waiters had also brought up bottles of Belfast sparkling cider. That was a kind of carbonated apple juice. All the old Chinese restaurants served it. We never had a Chinatown banquet without it. We used it to toast Mother. She beamed happily. Even Father forgot the waterfall and began to enjoy himself.

The other courses were just as good. There were huge platters of paper-wrapped chicken. Those were squares of chicken wrapped in parchment paper with sauces and spices and herbs. Then they were fried very quickly. That way the chicken stayed juicy and cooked inside the parchment.

The steamed fish came in a black bean sauce. Father took the fish cheeks, which he said were the tastiest.

"I wanted those," Uncle Mat complained.

"You snooze. You lose," Father said, chomping away happily. "Hmm, that is so good."

Uncle Mat reached over with his chopsticks and pried an eyeball from the socket. Setting it between his teeth, he leaned over toward Father. "I see you," he said.

Father leaned away. "Stop that. That's disgusting." If he thought Uncle Mat was bad, he ought to see his youngest son in action.

Uncle Mat was like a small boy. Once he knew he could bug someone, he played his trick on others. Springing to his feet, he started going around and shoving his face against other people's. At the same time, he made noises in his throat that sounded like "I see you."

Finally he tried that at Grandmother's table. She rapped him on the head with a knuckle. "Don't play with your food."

Uncle Mat swallowed the eyeball as he stood up. "Ow, that hurt," he said, rubbing his head.

"Come on. You can escort me. That should keep you out of a mischief for a while," Grandmother said, setting her napkin on the table. "That water-fall's gotten to me again."

Uncle Curtis taught school. He pried out the other eyeball. "Bobby," he asked, "did you know that the octopus eye is a lot like a human's?"

Bobby perked up. "Then it must only have one lens. Did you know that a cockroach eye has two thousand lenses?"

"No kidding," Uncle Curtis said, impressed.

I didn't want Bobby talking about bugs at the dinner table. That might lead to Arnie and Hercules. I knew Father would not be as under-standing as Charlie.

"Bucket time," I said. By now the new bucket was nearly flowing over.

"Bucket time." Aunt Martha took up the call, and the cry spread through the room.

Father frowned. "Paying customers shouldn't have to do this. Where's that waiter?" He twisted around and searched for one.

From her table, Grandmother saw Uncle Curtis playing with the other eyeball. "Curtis, you can switch the buckets this time. That should keep you from playing with your food."

"Aw, Mama," Uncle Curtis said, but he got up.

"Faster than a speeding plumber." Uncle Mat chuckled.

"And they make more than Curtis, too," Father laughed.

"But they don't have the love and admiration I get," Uncle Curtis said. However, he didn't have as much practice as the owner. When he switched the buckets, the water sloshed all over his shoes and pants.

That led to a lot more teasing from everyone.

There were lots more dishes, each better than the last one. So everyone was willing to put up with cries of "Bucket time." The only one who seemed to really mind was Father. At each course, he asked the waiter to do something about the buckets, and each time the waiter got more and more snippy.

By the time the prawn course came, we had used up the last empty bucket. All that was left was a row of full buckets.

The prawn dish was a specialty of the restaurant. They left the antennae on and arranged them so the prawns seemed to be dancing together in the center.

"They look an awful lot like crickets," I whispered uncomfortably to Bobby.

"Actually," Uncle Curtis said, "they're distant relations. Prawns are arthropods."

"Like spiders?" Bobby asked. He knew some real hundred-dollar words.

I thought of Madeline and lost my appetite.

The information didn't keep either Uncle Curtis or Bobby from tucking into the prawns. Father was the only other person who didn't eat. He was too busy twisting around looking for someone to take care of the full buckets. "Get the owner," he said to the waiter.

The waiter nodded as he grunted and left.

"It's his floor," Uncle Mat told Father. "He doesn't want it to get warped by water. He'll take care of it."

"But on Chinese time or American time?" Father complained.

"Who cares?" Uncle Mat said. "Try to learn to relax."

The prawns were halfway gone by the time the owner showed up. "You wanted to see me, sir?" he asked Father.

"Someone's got to empty the old buckets and bring them back," Father pointed.

"Yes, of course," the owner said. "I'll take care of it myself." I guess he knew better than to ask his waiters to do it.

"See, I knew it'd get taken care of," Uncle Mat said, as he reached into the bowl with his chopsticks. He brought out a brown object clutched between the chopstick tips. "Hmm, a mushroom."

Tilting back his head, he opened his mouth wide. He looked like a small bird being fed a worm.

Aunt Martha leaned forward and peered into the bowl. "That's funny. There shouldn't be mushrooms in this dish."

Father glanced sideways and then took a better look. "It's an awfully hairy mushroom."

"You're not talking me out of this," Uncle Mat said. "You snooze, you lose." He was enjoying beating Father to a tidbit for once. He held out the mushroom. "Don't you wish you had it?"

Father's eyes widened. "No."

"Liar," Uncle Mat said as he popped it into his mouth.

"Because those aren't hairs. Those were legs," Father said. "And they're moving."

From the corner of my eye, I saw Bobby searching his pockets frantically. Suddenly he looked very pale.

"What's wrong?" I whispered.

"The lid came off the ink box," Bobby whispered.

I clamped a hand over his mouth. I didn't want him shouting that Uncle Mat was eating Hercules.

However, the others at the table figured out what it was at the same time we did. "It's a cockroach," Uncle Mat said, spitting. The bug shot like a bullet across the table.

Arnie and I weren't the only ones afraid of cockroach cooties. Suddenly everyone was on their feet and shouting and screaming. It's funny how quickly the commotion spread. Even though Hercules was at our table, people at the other tables started jumping up and yelling, too. You'd have thought an army of cockroaches had suddenly invaded the room.

Plates, glasses, cups, and bowls crashed to the floor as Uncle Mat tried to swat Hercules. Then Uncle Curtis started in. Father was the strongest and the angriest.

Bobby knocked a plate off the table as he stretched out his hands. "No, don't."

Grabbing Bobby, I pulled him back.

"Got it," Father said. He inspected his palm with satisfaction.

"It's too late," I whispered in his ear.

The owner came running over. "What are you doing?"

Father held out his hand. "Killing the bugs in your restaurant. What kind of place is this? Broken pipes and now bugs."

The owner's eyebrows shot up. "What's a cockroach doing here?" He began to slap at the table the hardest of all. "I can assure you. We run the cleanest place in town. The Health Department never has a problem here."

"Poor Hercules," Bobby murmured.

He was the only one mourning.

Eleven

Uncle Mat was still in shock. He just sat there staring at the prawn dish. It didn't help that the buglike prawns stared back.

The owner was all over Papa. "I'm so sorry. This has never happened before. I run a clean place."

"You don't have cockroaches or waterfalls in good restaurants." Papa pointed at the column of water. "Customers shouldn't have to take care of your bugs or your plumbing mistakes."

"Yes, you're right. I'm so sorry again. I'll talk to

the waiters." He grinned nervously. "So you don't have to mention it to anyone, right?"

"I wouldn't let my friends go through this." Father nodded first to the prawn dish and then to the waterfall.

"It won't ever happen again." The owner took a handkerchief. He mopped his forehead. "And you've been such good customers. So, of course, there's no charge for the meal."

That really surprised Father. "Well . . ." he said thoughtfully.

Uncle Curtis snapped his fingers. "We should have ordered more sparkling cider."

The owner spread his arms out wide. "Of course, more cider for everyone."

Father patted the frozen Uncle Mat on his shoulder. "And maybe something stronger for Mat. He was the one who found the surprise."

"Of course, of course," the owner said, nodding. He brought up the new bottles personally and took care of the water buckets.

Everyone enjoyed the bubbly soda. Even Uncle Mat became his old sunny self after the owner brought him a special drink.

However, the prawn dishes went untouched. Everyone was scared of more uninvited "mushrooms."

Only Bobby didn't drink the soda. He sat looking sad and small.

I slung my arm around him and whispered, "Don't worry. We'll find another by tomorrow. And if we don't, I know a way to stay out of Arnie's way."

The next day we could hide in the chapel. Arnie wouldn't beat us up there. And if we hid there, Bobby couldn't bother me with bug talk. He'd have to keep his mouth shut while we were there.

"But Hercules is gone," Bobby said.

It finally dawned on me. My little brother was mourning a dead cockroach. I could just picture him years from now. He'd be like Charlie, wandering around in an apartment filled with bugs. And as happy as a bug in a rug.

Worried, I warned him, "You're getting to be as weird as the Bug Lady."

"Okay, okay. Don't get mad," he squeaked hastily.

I drew my eyebrows together puzzled. "Why would I get mad?"

He laughed nervously. "I don't know."

Suddenly it hit me. "You think I'm just like Arnie, don't you? I don't lose my temper like that."

His eyes started growing bigger. "No, not at all."

"I don't hit you." But I realized that my hug had turned into a headlock. "Much."

"You're my brother. It's okay," he said simply. That was enough explanation for him.

"Boys," Mother scolded.

"We were just playing," I said, letting go.

"Yeah, just playing," Bobby agreed.

I didn't want to be another Arnie. So instead of staying mad, I tried to see what Bobby saw in Hercules. Though I strained my brain, I couldn't. "You actually miss that cockroach, don't you?" I asked puzzled.

"As much as Oscar," he confessed.

I hadn't understood how he had liked Oscar the alligator, either. Alligators aren't affectionate pets. They're only interested in one thing: their next meal.

I stared at Bobby for a moment. There were a lot of puzzles in life. Where does the second sock disappear to when you wash them? How do hangers multiply in the closet?

Little brothers, though, were the biggest mystery of all. Exploring outer space was easier than exploring the inner space between Bobby's ears.

"I know you hated Hercules," Bobby sniffed, "but he didn't hate you. We were giants to him. He trusted us. He thought we'd protect him." He shook his head, ashamed. "But we didn't."

I scratched my cheek. I had never thought of myself as being a giant anything. "What do you think I looked like to him?"

Bobby stretched his hands high over his head. "Maybe a big tower or a fort."

For a moment, I could almost picture myself as tall as a mountain—or more likely a dangerous volcano that rumbled a lot.

Sometimes I felt like I had put on magical glasses when I talked to Bobby. "You know something weird?" I confessed. "I can almost see what Hercules saw."

"It's fascinating, isn't it?" he asked eagerly.

How often had my little brother said that about something? Lots.

How often did I say that? Never.

Bobby could take pleasure in anything and everything. He could watch a weed growing from a crack in the sidewalk or a raindrop on his palm.

Me? I just stepped on the weeds and complained about getting wet in the rain.

Perhaps I wasn't so smart after all.

I don't think I was ever going to like bugs. However, if I survived Arnie, maybe I'd even try to look at things more like Bobby.

Bobby kicked his legs guiltily against his chair. "Maybe we should tell them about Hercules."

As smart as Bobby was, he didn't know everything. "What's the point? You heard Father. The owner should never have put us up here with the leaking pipes. Now shut up."

Since the restaurant didn't have desserts, Aunt Norma had brought a big cake in a pink box. On the white icing were little plastic palm trees. The words were NEXT TIME TAKE HER TO HAWAII. HAPPY BIRTHDAY ANYWAY.

That got a big laugh from everyone except Father. "Ha, ha, ha," Father chuckled anxiously.

"So don't be cheap," Aunt Ethel scolded. "You

can use the money you saved from the banquet. That should help buy part of the tickets."

Mother came to Father's defense. "He's not cheap. He spends a lot of money on us. He just doesn't want to close up the store."

"You're the best in Chinatown," Uncle Mat said. "Don't be afraid of the competition. Your customers will be waiting by your door when you come back."

"Maybe," Father said unhappily.

There was only one candle for Mother. "We don't want you wearing yourself out," Aunt Norma said. She'd also brought paper plates and plastic forks.

The cake was chocolate with vanilla icing. Bobby and I each got corner pieces with double icing. In my book, the cake was the hit of the party. Even though he was unhappy, Bobby polished off his piece, too.

Uncle Mat had three pieces. When his wife, Aunt Martha, shot him a dirty look, he insisted, "It helps my nerves."

Afterward, we helped Mother carry her presents home.

"I'm not cheap," Father murmured.

"No, of course you're not," Mother said. "We live very comfortably."

"We'll go to Hawaii some time," Father insisted.

"I'd rather go to Disneyland," I said.

"You don't get to vote," Father said.

Maybe it's just as well. If Bobby got to vote, we'd wind up at some place educational rather than fun—like the museum of toasters.

So he surprised me when he suggested, "Hawaii would be nice."

"You can't even swim," I said in surprise.

"You don't need to swim to have fun," Bobby said.

"How big are the bugs in Hawaii?" I asked him suspiciously.

Mother said, "I hear they're pretty big." She gave a shudder. "Especially the cockroaches."

Suddenly I knew why Bobby wanted to visit there. "Hawaii has waterfalls, too," I reminded Father.

Father gave a grunt. "But their waterfalls don't come from busted pipes. They're all natural."

Twelve

When we got to our apartment house, I wrinkled my nose. Mr. Wong was brewing some more of his medicines. The smell hung over the hallway. Father fished out his keys. "If Mr. Wong brewed his medicines at the restaurant, they'd never have to worry about bugs."

"Or humans," I said, holding my nose.

"Shhh." Mother shushed us. "He'll hear you."

Father sighed with relief when he opened the door. "That's a little more excitement than I want with a meal."

Mother seemed glad to be home, too. "You

like a floor show when we eat out," she giggled.

"I want the dancers to have two legs, not eight," Father said.

"Actually, it's six," Bobby corrected him.

I motioned for him to be quiet.

"Now let's let Mother unwrap her loot," Father said.

"Let me get the knife from the kitchen," Mother said.

I groaned. Unwrapping gifts with Mother was less fun than it sounded. For one thing, she tried to save all the paper.

Half the fun of getting a present is tearing off the wrapping. And unfortunately Bobby took after Mother. Unwrapping Christmas presents took forever.

From Uncle Mat and Aunt Martha, Mother got slippers in the shape of hairy feet. "How . . . nice," she said, trying to find something good to say. "I bet these will be real warm."

Father set them aside. "Mat must have done the shopping again this year."

"Well, Martha is very busy with her beauty parlor," Mother said.

Most of the other presents were normal and very, very boring. Mother got blouses, scarves, soap, and other terribly practical things. What's the point of getting something you could buy any day for yourself? At least, our present showed imagination.

When Mother had gone through her other presents, Father went to a drawer. "And this one's from me," Father said, lifting out a pretty box.

It turned out to be a lime-green raincoat. "I hope you like it," Father said.

Mother pulled at the shoulders to test the seams. Then she looked at the stitches. "It's very well made."

"See. I'm not cheap," Father insisted.

Mother gave him a quick hug. "I never said you were. Don't pay any attention to Ethel. She was just teasing you."

Bobby went over to another drawer. "Here's our present, Mother," he said eagerly.

We had wounds lots of tape around the stem last night. Then I'd cut up a pink paper bag and used that for wrapping.

"It's from both of us," I said, handing it to her.

Mother examined the long, thin package. "I wonder what it is."

"We're not telling," Bobby warned her.

"No matter how much I tickle you?" Mother asked.

Bobby was firm. "Nope."

Even Mother had to admit defeat with our package. Her knife couldn't cut all the tape we had put on it. Finally she just started ripping.

"Isn't that more satisfying?" I asked her.

Mother leaned her head to the side. "I guess it is. But we can always use the paper."

We had a closet full of recycled wrapping paper. You name the holiday, and we had something for it. Mother knew her paper like librarians know their books.

She had attacked our package from the top. Even so, she had trouble tearing apart the tape that we had wound around the present's outside. "I wonder what it is," she murmured to herself.

Finally, she could see the hand in the opening. It almost looked like a flower in the paper. "What is that?" she asked with a laugh.

"Careful," Bobby warned anxiously.

"We . . . had a little accident getting it home," I added.

Slowly Mother pulled the back scratcher from the package. "Just what I need," she said.

Bobby sighed. "We weren't sure."

"And I just have this itch," Mother said. She lifted the back scratcher over her shoulder and angled the hand down. However, the moment she tried to scratch, the back scratcher snapped.

"It's the thought that counts," Mother said, hugging first me and then Bobby. "Thank you, boys."

Father started to pick up the gift boxes. "I'll take these into the bedr—" Suddenly, with a shout, he dropped all of them.

"What's wrong?" Mother asked.

Father began stamping his foot at the floor. "Bug, bug."

Bobby leaned forward and then grabbed my arm. "That's Hercules," he whispered. "He must have gotten out of my pocket here."

"It must have been another cockroach at the restaurant," I said.

Hercules had picked the wrong woman to

tangle with. Mother grabbed a can of insect spray from a bureau and began to spray gray mist over everything.

At the same time, Father kept stomping. "Don't worry. I got it. I got it."

"No, please," Bobby said. He started toward Mother, but she held up a hand.

"Stand back, Bobby," she warned.

I grabbed Bobby. "You heard Mother."

"But—" Bobby began to protest.

I covered up his mouth. "You'd better keep your mouth closed. You don't want to breathe in those fumes."

"I hate bugs," Mother said, continuing to spray.

"Ha!" Father said as he gave one final, terrible stamp.

Thirteen

Our parents got out the sponges and buckets and disinfectants. They weren't going to have any cockroach cooties in their home.

As they cleaned up, I guided Bobby to the bathroom. Bobby didn't say anything. He just moved like a zombie.

Poor kid. He'd gone through the shock of losing Hercules not once but twice in the same evening.

My parents had the right idea. Since we'd also been in Charlie's place, we might be covered by more than cockroach cooties.

So I filled the bathtub with hot water. Because I

100

felt sorry for Bobby, I let him use the water first. Usually I got the tub first because that's one of my rights as the oldest (and biggest). Then I put all our clothes in the hamper for the dirty laundry.

As we got ready for bed, I began to worry about him. "We'll be okay."

Bobby was a real worrywart. "What are we going to do without our bodyguard?"

I plumped my pillow into a more comfortable shape. "We'll hide in the chapel."

Bobby snapped off the light. "I'm sorry to be so much trouble."

Well, he was, but I didn't want to pick on him after losing his pet bug. "You chased Arnie away today."

I heard Bobby climb into bed. "But I may not be able to tomorrow. I wanted to take care of things for a change."

"Don't worry," I assured him. "I'll get us out of this mess. I always find a way, don't I?"

Bobby's voice floated out of the darkness. In the distance, I could hear our parents preparing for bed. "I know you can, but you're always taking care of things for us."

"I'm older than you," I said. "What do you expect?"

"But you shouldn't have to," he said. "That's the point."

I felt guilty over the harsh things I had said. "Why do you want to try?" I asked.

"Because you're my brother," he said simply.

I rested my head on my pillow. "I guess that's why I do it, too." I sighed.

"Do you really want to hide from Arnie?" he asked.

I pulled the covers up around my neck. "No, but I don't see what choice we have. We can't fight that goon," I said. "I guess kids are going to think we're getting holy. We'll be spending all our time near the nuns or in the chapel."

"But," Bobby asked slowly, "what if we could outsmart him?"

I saw one fatal flaw in that scheme. "Arnie is smarter than you think."

Bobby snapped his fingers. "Hey! Do you still have those cookies?"

I'd been so full of cake that I had forgotten my other treats. "What cookies?" I asked innocently.

"The ones you took from Charlie," Bobby said, "even though I warned you not to."

"You're not nearly as dumb as you look," I grumbled.

Bobby's bedsprings *boing*ed, and suddenly he snapped on the light.

I shaded my eyes against the brightness. "What are you doing?"

Bobby padded on bare feet over to my jacket. "Give them to me."

Annoyed, I threw off my covers and started to get up. "Not a chance. That's my snack for tomorrow."

Bobby already had his hands in my jacket pocket. "Do you want to get Arnie off our backs forever?"

"Who wouldn't?" I admitted.

"Then I need these cookies," Bobby said. He found a paper bag and put them into it. "Tomorrow we're going to bring our own lunches."

"But tomorrow the cafeteria serves hot dogs and spaghetti again," I said. That had been the one thing I had looked forward to.

Bobby sighed. "How can you think of your stomach after that big meal we just had?"

I patted my stomach. "It's easy. I'm a growing boy."

"Bring a sandwich tomorrow. I promise you we'll have Arnie off our backs." Bobby took the bag with him to bed as a precaution.

"Give those cookies back," I demanded angrily.

"I'm not going to eat them. They're part of the plan," Bobby said.

I started to get out of bed. When Bobby got pigheaded, I usually bounced him around a little. He always came to his senses after that. But I was being just like Arnie again. So I rolled back into bed. It was really annoying.

When we snapped off the light, I listened suspiciously for the sound of munching. However, all Bobby said was, "Don't worry. I won't let anything happen to you."

Of all things today and tonight, that was the weirdest. All my life I had been the big brother and he had been the little pest. "What are you going to do?" I demanded.

"You don't want to know. Trust me," he said. And soon he was snoring. He didn't seem to have a care in the world anymore. What did he have up his sleeve? I didn't expect it to work—any more than I expected him to fly. I'd been stupid to think Bobby might be right about anything. My brother was just plain crazy.

The only trouble was that I didn't have *any* solution to the Arnie problem. I tossed and turned all night.

Arnie was going to demolish me.

Fourteen

The next morning I woke Bobby early. "We've got to find another bug," I said.

He sat up, blinking his eyes sleepily. "There'll never be another Hercules."

I could have argued with him, but the goal was to scare away Arnie. "Yeah, right. Now come on."

We got dressed quickly and then tried to go outside. The moment we opened the door, though, we started to cough.

Our apartment reeked of bug spray. Mother was already in the kitchen. The floor was littered with plates and cans and odd appliances. She had her head inside a cabinet as she sprayed.

"Is that safe?" I asked.

"I've got to get every crack and crevice," she said as she coughed.

Gloomily I realized that our apartment was cockroach- and cootie-free. We were stuck with hiding in the chapel.

Bobby picked his way through the debris to the refrigerator. "Do we have stuff for sandwiches?"

Mother pulled her head out of the cabinet. "But the cafeteria serves your favorite lunch today. It's not like it's liver."

Bobby shrugged. "We're bored. We want something different."

Mother scratched her forehead. "There's not much to eat in the apartment. Let's see what we have."

Washing her hands, she found two pieces of cheese. The corners had dried like linoleum, but we trimmed them off. The bread wasn't much better. "Is that mold?" Mother wondered. She held the slices by the light to study them.

At that moment, I lost heart in my little brother's scheme. "That's okay. I guess we can eat in the cafeteria after all." I could feel my taste buds jump for joy.

"They'll be great toasted," Bobby said.

"Yeah, then we can't tell why they're hard," I said gloomily.

Father came in with a rolled-up newspaper. His eyes darted all around the room. "Find anything?"

Mother nodded to a lemon yellow object on the floor. "No bugs, but I did find that. Do you know what it is? I think it was a wedding present."

Father squatted over it and yanked at the electrical cord. "Well, it must be some kind of appliance. It can use electricity."

"But I couldn't find any opening," Mother said.

Father looked at the scrap of paper that had been taped to the side. "It's from Curtis. Maybe we can ask him what it is."

Mother shuddered. "And get a lecture for an hour?"

Father nudged an avocado-green machine. "What's this for?"

"I was hoping you'd know," Mother said. "The note says you got it for your thirtieth birthday."

Father poked it. "I bet it's from Curtis, too."

Mother waved a hand at another half-dozen mystery objects. "All of them must be. I wonder if he knocked some things together at school just to tease us."

"Well, what's this?" Father picked up a metal thing with a lot of gears. When he turned the crank, the gears moved musically.

"Don't get it too near your hair," Mother warned with a laugh.

He looked at the handle, he read the label. "It's a Handy Dandy."

"But for what?" Mother laughed.

"I don't know. Haircuts maybe?" He felt the sides of his head.

While Mother and Father were trying to figure out the appliances, Bobby took over the lunch preparations. After he put the bread into the toaster, he whispered to me, "I know what I'm doing, Teddy. Don't worry."

"Maybe I wouldn't worry if you told me," I said in a low voice.

"Well . . ." Bobby suddenly shut his mouth.

"Why can't you just tell me?" I demanded.

"I just can't," he said. He looked guilty.

He squirmed uncomfortably. "Just let me handle this," he said. "And Arnie will be out of our hair for a while."

Suddenly I got suspicious. I never knew what my weird little brother was going to do. "You're not going to poison him, are you?"

Bobby looked insulted. "I wouldn't hurt anyone." Then he grinned. "At least, not exactly."

Leaning against the counter, he hummed to himself as he waited for the bread to toast. He was off in his own world again.

Exasperated, I helped Bobby make the sandwiches and put them into paper bags. I wasn't going to depend on my weirdo brother, though. I had my own plan, lousy as it was.

When we left, Mother and Father were still experimenting with the mystery appliances. They were giggling like two kids with new toys.

Outside our apartment, Bobby took the bag with Charlie's cookies from his jacket pocket. He slipped half of them into each of our lunch bags.

"Whatever you do, don't eat these," Bobby said.

"Why not?" I asked as we started down the hall-way. "What's wrong with them?"

"Just don't eat them," Bobby said.

I'd about had it with him. I couldn't fight the Arnie-zilla in me anymore. And we were out of our parents' hearing now. "Tell me." I balled my fingers into a fist.

Bobby started to back away. He knew the signs when I was about to blow my top. "But you aren't a very good liar."

"I am too," I shot back—though I wasn't sure I wanted to win this argument.

"Just follow my lead," Bobby said, beginning to run.

I went after him, but years of being chased had made my little brother quick.

When I saw the green-tiled roof of our school in the distance, my stomach tightened. I hadn't liked Hercules. However, he'd been our only defense against Arnie. Fear of Arnie replaced anger at Bobby. "Slow down, Bobby," I called. "I won't hit you. Stick with me."

Bobby, on the other hand, didn't look worried at

all. "Just follow my lead," he shouted as he joined the stream of students.

"You don't want to go in blind," I said desperately.

However, my little brother plunged down the hill with the others before I could stop him.

My little brother was bent on suicide. Well, that wasn't my problem, was it? Except he thought he was doing it for me, too.

Against my better judgment, I went after him.

Fifteen

"**C**ome back," I called, forcing my way through the others.

As soon as he heard me, Bobby turned and started talking up a storm. "I can't wait until we have lunch. Can you, Teddy?" He arched his eyebrows. He wanted me to pick up my cue.

"Yeah, whatever," I said, waving frantically for him to come back.

So he tried to do the work for the two of us. He did a real good job. By the time we reached school, my stomach was growling.

"What have you got in your lunch bag?" Ollie asked.

"Well, you know our mother had a birthday banquet last night," Bobby said loudly. He rubbed his stomach. "It sure was good." He glanced back at me.

"Well, what you got in the bag?" Ollie asked. He tried to peer into Bobby's sack.

However, Bobby switched the bag into his other hand. That way his body shielded his lunch. "Get lost."

Ollie turned his attention to me. "Come on, Teddy," he wheedled. "You're going to share with your pal, aren't you?"

I was glad to have a target for my frustration at last. I shoved Ollie away—maybe a little harder than I should have. "Scram."

"See if I ever share anything with you," Ollie grumbled. Opening his lunch bag, he took out an apple and began to munch it unhappily.

I noticed that others who had been in earshot were also snacking early on their lunches. Maybe Bobby could get a job doing commercials.

"Come back," I whispered as I made a grab for him.

Bobby dodged away. "I know what I'm doing."

Surrounded by munching schoolmates, he began to walk the last block to school. Streams of students flowed in from other directions so we were in a solid uniformed river. Towering over the others, I saw Arnie-zilla. He was drawing a finger across his throat and grinning at me.

"Bobby," I said.

He ignored me as he kept right on talking.

I tried to get to him, but there were too many people in my way.

"Ow," someone yelled.

"Quit it," someone else complained.

I twisted my head around. Arnie was tromping through the crowd toward me like Godzilla stomping through Tokyo.

"Bobby," I said frantically.

All I could do was follow him down the metal stairs into the courtyard. Bobby began to really pour it on about our lunches. In the rotunda above the stairs, his voice echoed as if he had an amplifier.

Suddenly someone grabbed my collar and jerked me to a halt. "I've been looking for you two," Arnie said.

Instantly everyone began to panic. They flowed around Arnie and me as if we were rocks in a river.

I looked desperately toward the courtyard, but there wasn't a nun in sight. And in a moment, we were all alone. And Arnie in all his fury was between us and the chapel. Arnie was going to pulverize us. This was a fine mess Bobby had gotten us into.

I licked my lips. "Can't we talk about this?" I asked desperately.

"Sure." He held up a fist. "I let this do my talking."

"Arnie! Your fight's really with me, not with Teddy." Bobby stood at the foot of the stairs. I'd never seen anyone do anything that brave.

Arnie grinned wickedly. "Today, I've got a special deal. Two beatings for the price of one."

Bobby smiled pleasantly. "Then start with me first. But I'll warn you. Your arms are just going to get tired. I can take a lot."

"We'll see," Arnie said, and set me on my feet on a step.

I stumbled down the steps to Bobby. "Get out of here, Bobby."

Bobby put down his book bag but handed his lunch to me. "Hide this."

If the cookies were our secret weapon, I couldn't see any reason for it. "But—" I began to protest.

"Don't argue. Just do it," he hissed as he thrust the lunch bag at me.

I was so surprised that I dropped my own book bag with a loud noise. Bobby never lost his temper. That's why everyone liked him.

Shocked, I took his lunch bag. At his nod, I hid mine behind me as well.

As a bully, Arnie was a real artist. Your average bully would just start hitting you. However, that wasn't enough for Arnie. He wanted to prolong the humiliation.

Leaning his head to the side, he jerked his head at me. "What's in the bags?"

"It's nothing. Just some cheese sandwiches," Bobby said quickly.

"Yeah?" Arnie said skeptically. "I heard you yakking about your lunches."

Bobby shook his head. "You really don't want them."

117

"You can't even lie good," Arnie snorted and held out a hand.

I didn't know what to do. For once, I was the helpless one. I . . . needed Bobby. That was an odd sensation. Bobby wasn't the little pest anymore. I wound up looking desperately at him. He nodded his head.

Silently I handed the lunches over to Arnie. Opening one of the sacks, he shoved his hand in. His grin faded as he held up the sandwich. Unwrapping it, he peered between the slices of toast. "It really is cheese," he said and sniffed it. "And old cheese, too."

I could feel the sweat breaking out all over me. Bobby, though, was a real cool customer. "I told you," he said as he held out his hand.

However, Arnie threw the cheese sandwich onto the ground. He took out the other sandwich. "More old cheese," he muttered after he inspected it. He dumped it as well. "I didn't think anyone was as bad as my mother, but yours is even worse."

It was the first I knew that Arnie had a mother. I always thought he'd come from the ocean like Godzilla.

"Our mother's just fine," I said angrily, but Bobby shook his head at me to be quiet.

I was so desperate that I had to let Bobby do things his way. It was not only scary, but it was downright unnatural. The next thing I knew the sun would be rising in the west.

"There's got to be something." He shook the bags. The cookies rattled inside. The grin slowly returned. "I told you that you couldn't fool me."

Opening a sack, he took out the chocolate chip cookies. "These look pretty good." He nibbled at one. "It's a little different." He took another bite. "But tasty."

I watched in annoyance as he wolfed down a handful of my treats. Some plan of Bobby's.

When Arnie emptied the other sack, he threw both of them on the ground. Rubbing his palms against one another, he dusted off the crumbs. "Not bad. Now for the real dessert." He balled both hands into fists.

Bobby, though, sat down on a step. "How do you feel?" he asked in his best scientific voice.

Arnie shrugged. "Just fine."

Bobby tapped his stomach. "No tickling in there?"

"Just a full belly," Arnie said, patting his tummy.

Bobby leaned back on the stairs, resting on his elbows. He looked back at me. "I guess it takes a little while longer."

"What takes longer?" Arnie asked suspiciously.

Bobby took a notebook and pen out of his book bag. "You know where we live?" he asked Arnie.

Arnie jerked his head. "Sure."

Bobby found a blank page. "You know the funny apartment next to us?"

Suddenly Arnie didn't look so confident. "The one with all the bugs in the window? Who doesn't? It's the talk of Chinatown."

Bobby wrote EXPERIMENT in big letters. "Well, those cookies were baked by her."

Arnie craned his neck so he could read the word. "They're just chocolate chip cookies," he said.

Bobby shook his head. "Wrong."

"I tasted the chocolate chips myself," Arnie snapped.

Bobby tapped the pen against his lips. "Know what the full name for the recipe is?"

"What?" Arnie demanded.

I wanted to know myself. It was like watching a horror movie. I knew some monster was hiding behind the door, but I wanted to see it anyway.

"Buggy Buddies," Bobby said, and poised his pen over the page. "How do you feel?"

"You're joking, right?" Arnie asked, shocked.

"All of Charlie's desserts have bugs in them," Bobby said.

Suddenly my legs felt real wobbly. I'd come that close to eating them myself.

Arnie began to feel his stomach. "I ate bugs?"

"Prime grade-A," Bobby assured him, and took a note.

"But they were dead, right," Arnie said shakily. "I mean, they were cut up small. They had to be."

"But if one of them had eggs . . ." Bobby paused and sighed. "Charlie tries to screen them, but she doesn't always get the eggs. They're so tiny."

Arnie clutched one of the railings. "What happens if you do?"

Bobby studied Arnie and then made another note. "Sometimes they hatch."

"Oh, no." Arnie sat down heavily beside Bobby.

Bobby leaned over to peer at Arnie's stomach. "Nope. Nothing yet." He made another notation.

Arnie suddenly grabbed Bobby. "What happens next?"

My little brother smiled sweetly. "They eat their way out."

Sixteen

Arnie stretched his mouth wide. I thought he was going to scream. However, his chest began to move in and out, and all that came out were little sobs. It sounded like there was a tiny baby lost inside of his big body. He slumped against a wall and sat down.

Suddenly I felt dizzy. I plopped down next to him.

There were worse things than cockroach cooties. And Bobby had set Arnie up. I didn't think my sweet little brother had it in him. It might be smarter to be nicer to him—if I could stand it.

Arnie whirled around and grabbed me in his huge paws. "What'll I do?" Tears began to streak his face. "You got to tell me what to do," he demanded over and over. He started to shake me.

"I d-d-on't k-know," I said as he rocked me back and forth.

"You got to help me," Arnie blubbered. "Get me to the hospital. I don't want to die."

Bobby squatted in front of us. He put a hand on Arnie's shoulders. "It's okay," he said gently.

Arnie stopped shaking me, but he still gripped my shirt. "But I got bugs in me. I hate bugs."

"There weren't any eggs in those bugs," Bobby said. "And even if there were, the baking would kill them. There's nothing to worry about."

It was strange to see little Bobby comforting big Arnie.

"Yeah?" Arnie asked.

"Yeah," Bobby said, nodding his head for emphasis.

Arnie took a deep breath. "I hate cockroaches."

"Cockroaches are neat," Bobby insisted.

Arnie gave a shudder. "You wouldn't say that if you woke up and found them crawling all over you. All those tiny legs tickling you. And covering you with cockroach cooties. Once I opened my mouth to cry and one of them dropped in my mouth. I spit it out, but that's when they really started to give me the creeps."

"I like bugs, but not inside me," Bobby agreed.

"Well, they're all over our apartment, still," Arnie said. "When I open the door, I keep my eyes shut and count to a hundred. By then, most of them have run out of sight."

"Our mom would have been spraying and spraying," I said, remembering Mom this morning. And that had only been one bug.

"My mom's says she's no maid and no cook." Arnie paused and then laughed bitterly. "She's not into being a mom, period."

I remembered yesterday when he heard we were buying a present for our mother. Had he been jealous? Was that why he had broken our present?

"What about your father?" I asked.

Arnie wiped his tears away. "That jerk? He split a long time ago."

It sounded like he was on his own. "I didn't know."

Arnie glared at me. "Don't get the wrong idea about my mom. She works at two jobs. She's a waitress during the day. Then she cleans for most of the night. When she comes home, she's only got a few hours to sleep."

"So you hardly ever see her," Bobby said.

I stared at my little brother, puzzled. Suddenly I realized what Bobby was doing. If he could see things through Hercules' eyes, he could also see them through Arnie's as well. Well, maybe that wasn't such a big leap from a cockroach to Arnie-zilla.

So I tried it myself. I wondered what it would be like with no father and almost no mother. He had no one to get rid of the bugs like our parents did. Or protect us.

If I grew up on my own, I guess I'd have to be pretty tough, too. I might even turn out like Arnie. That thought was as scary as the bugs.

Arnie drew his knees up against his chest and hugged them. "So it was a trick?"

"I'm sorry," Bobby said. "You didn't give us a choice."

Arnie sniffed. "So why didn't you get the other kids? You all could have a good laugh."

Bobby sat down. "That's what I planned to do." He leaned back on his hands. "But then I couldn't."

"Why not?" Arnie asked suspiciously. "I would have."

So would I.

"The kids would have made fun of me. No one would have been scared of me anymore," Arnie said.

"You've already had it tough enough," Bobby said.

Arnie's head snapped back angrily. "Don't you feel sorry for me. I'd get my reputation back." He held up his fists. "I still got these."

Bobby raised and lowered his shoulders. "And you'd begin with Teddy and me. And we'd be right back where we started. So what's the point? We just want you to stop picking on us."

"Is that all?" Arnie asked.

"Just leave us alone," I said.

"And you'd keep your mouths shut about this?" Arnie asked hopefully.

Bobby looked at me. I was the older brother after all. "What do you think, Teddy?"

127

That was a lot easier than living in the chapel the rest of my life.

"You've got our word," I promised. "So do we have a peace treaty?"

Arnie stuck out a paw. "Yeah."

Bobby's hand disappeared in his. I put my hand over theirs and we shook hands.

Suddenly I heard a growling from someone's stomach. "Do you have any money?" Bobby asked me.

"Not a dime," I admitted.

Turning, Bobby started to pick up the cheese sandwich.

"I'll clean up the trash," Arnie said. "I don't want any reminders laying around."

"This is our lunch for this afternoon," Bobby said. "We could throw away the dirty slice."

Arnie shrugged. "I'll share my lunch with you later."

"You will?" I asked surprised.

"It's only fair," Arnie said. Getting up, he got his books and a big brown bag. "And my cookies come wrapped from the factory."

Lunch with Arnie would be as interesting as

128

tea with Madeline. And maybe just as challenging.

I thought about asking the lunch ladies if I could give them an IOU instead. However, I wasn't sure how Arnie would take it. Would he get mad again if I refused his hospitality? So instead, I just gulped and said, "Thanks."

All that morning in our classes and at recess, the other kids treated us with kid gloves. They acted as if we had been hit by a locomotive. And we couldn't tell them the truth because of our promise to Arnie.

So when lunchtime finally rolled around everyone was surprised when we joined our enemy.

I could see heads twisting and people began to whisper and point at us. Usually Arnie sat by himself. Arnie ignored the attention though. He'd been getting into trouble ever since he had come to school. I guess he didn't care what people thought—so long as they thought he was tough.

The only problem was that there weren't three seats together. Arnie went up to a couple of kids. "Scram," he said, jerking a thumb.

Instantly they scurried away. Arnie sat down and patted a seat with a grin.

Arnie hadn't lost any of his temper. He was just going to aim it in a different direction.

When we had sat down, he opened that big brown bag. Out of it he lifted a box of ladyfinger cookies and a quart of milk.

"Your mother buys you that?" I asked.

Arnie laughed. "She just gives me the money. I buy what I like. And today I like these." He added, "I think I lost my taste for cookies, though."

I thought lunch might be one long silence. However, it turned out that he had seen as many Godzilla movies as we had. "What's your favorite?" he demanded.

"I like the one where he battles the other monsters," I said. "It's like watching wrestlers—except they can breathe fire."

"I hate that one," Arnie said.

I wasn't going to take that anymore. "Well then, have you seen the one where he takes on Ghidrah?"

Bobby held up both hands. "Yeah, the three-headed one. That's the best."

Arnie wriggled on the seat and shook his head violently. "That's the stupidest," he insisted.

"That's just your opinion," I shot back.

Arnie still had an easy trigger. "Are you saying I'm wrong?"

I didn't stop to think. I wasn't going to have my favorite movie be insulted. "No, but you're not right, either," I snapped.

He grabbed me by the collar. "Are you saying I'm stupid?"

"No," I choked out.

I could see his face. It was all red and angry. The old Arnie was ready to pound me flatter than Hercules. "I may not get A's in school like you, but I'm not stupid."

"Arnie!" Bobby said. He kept his hand on his lap while his other hand shielded it from the view of the other kids.

"What?" Arnie demanded in exasperation.

Bobby raised his fingers like antennae. He wriggled them at Arnie like a cockroach full of cooties.

Arnie swallowed as he remembered the peace treaty. His fingers straightened. "Sorry," he mumbled.

I straightened my shirt. "Forget it."

Bobby played the peacemaker again. "It was our

fault. We should have asked you why you like Godzilla."

Arnie pressed his lips together as he stared at the ceiling. "I never thought about that. Let's see." He spoke slowly. "Well, he's big, so he's clumsy." He added, "And no one explains the rules to him."

I could have said the same about Arnie. "Yeah, that makes sense."

"I told you. I'm not dumb." He took a long, deep swig from the milk carton.

I didn't think we'd ever be best buddies. Arnie was too much like a volcano. You never knew when he was going to explode. But he wasn't a monster, either.

Just another human being.

Like us.

Seventeen

I waited for Bobby after school. He came out with Arnie. "See you guys tomorrow. Lunch?"

Tomorrow was "Meat Surprise" in the cafeteria. So skipping it was no hardship. "We'll bring sandwiches this time," I said. Maybe one for Arnie, too.

"Right," Arnie said. With a wave, he swaggered off. Kids bumped each other, trying to get out of his way.

However, the Arnie-zilla act didn't fool me anymore. He was going home to a lonely apartment with just bugs for company. And he hated bugs.

Bobby must have been thinking the same thing.

133

"I wouldn't want to be him for a million dollars," he said.

"Not for a gazillion," I agreed.

Silently we turned around and climbed the steep hill toward home. At the intersection, we waited for the cable car to rumble past. A tourist leaned out dangerously to take our picture.

I made a face, but Bobby waved his hand with a smile. That was just like my little brother.

Then he turned around to look down the hill at the school. "Well." He sighed. "We made it through the day."

It finally hit me then. Bobby had done it. In his own odd, funny way, he'd saved us from Arnie.

"Thanks to you," I admitted.

"When there's trouble, we've got to help one another," Bobby said.

I leaned in close so no one else could hear us. "I didn't do anything. It was all your idea."

Bobby glanced at me from the corners of his eyes. "So you're not mad that I didn't tell you the plan?"

I guess Bobby wasn't so worthless after all. In fact, he came in handy sometimes.

"You saved us." I shrugged.

"Brothers protect one another," Bobby said simply.

"I guess we're all we've got," I admitted. At any rate, I was stuck with him. Just as he was stuck with me.

"But that's enough," Bobby said.

I started across the street. "You tricked me and Arnie pretty good," I said. I had to give credit where it was due. "I didn't think you had it in you." I added as an afterthought, "But I'm never playing poker with you."

"You haven't taught me how," Bobby said, running to join me.

I'd never get rid of my cockroach cooties, but I was definitely getting over the little-brother cooties.

"And I never will," I laughed, putting my arm around him.

I know it sounds funny to say. But after years of living with a pest, I had finally found a brother. It felt strange.

But it also felt good.

Acknowledgement

I wish to thank Susan Meyers for her thoughtful insights concerning this story based on her years working as a docent at the Insect Zoo at the San Francisco Zoo. Between her and Joanne, I have learned far more than I ever wanted to about bugs.